AT THE TWELFTH HOUR

Selected Short Stories of Joseph A. Altsheler

**Selected and with an Introduction by
Robert M. McIlvaine**

University Press of America,® Inc.
Lanham · Boulder · New York · Toronto · Plymouth, UK

Copyright © 2007 by
University Press of America,® Inc.
4501 Forbes Boulevard
Suite 200
Lanham, Maryland 20706
UPA Acquisitions Department (301) 459-3366

Estover Road
Plymouth PL6 7PY
United Kingdom

Library of Congress Control Number: 2007932052
ISBN-13: 978-0-7618-3859-3 (clothbound : alk. paper)
ISBN-10: 0-7618-3859-7 (clothbound : alk. paper)
ISBN-13: 978-0-7618-3860-9 (paperback : alk. paper)
ISBN-10: 0-7618-3860-0 (paperback : alk. paper)

For Wyatt, Isaac, and Owen

Three American Boys

Contents

Introduction, Part 1

The Fiction of Joseph A. Altsheler

ROBERT M. MCILVAINE

> If the boys like my books, tell them to read the history behind them—
> above all to read Parkman; he has been my great inspiration: Parkman
> has meant more to me than any other writer. (Moore, *Owls*, 322)

So spoke the most popular author of boys' fiction in the summer of
1918, the last year of his life. In that year he had been voted The
Most Popular Boys' Writer in America by a public libraries committee,
and he was being interviewed by Anne Carroll Moore, the superinten-
dent of Children's Work at the New York Public Library. Ms. Moore
wrote reviews of children's books for *The Bookman*, and Joseph Alexander
Altsheler was one of her favorite authors.

Altsheler (1862-1919) died soon after this interview, but his period
of great popularity lasted until at least World War II. A survey taken by
a Louisville, Kentucky school teacher in 1937 revealed that "seventy-
five percent of the boys and twenty per cent of the girls between the ages
of eleven and thirteen were Altsheler Readers." (Demaree 134) Anne
Carroll Moore attributed his popularity to the fact that after World War
I boys were looking for believable, truthful narratives, not "the old bluff,
bluster and braggadocio fostered by so many writers for boys." (Roads
27). She continued by writing, "Mr. Altsheler's popularity has been
greater in public libraries than that of any living writer for boys in the
past twenty years, and his influence has been broader than that of any

earlier writer for boys within my memory." (52,53) Altsheler stated that as a boy he had been influenced by the Waverly novels, Dickens, Thackeray, and Cooper, and "thrilling tales of Indians and pioneers handed down by word of mouth." (*Owls* 322) Moore added that "Beadle's dime novels were doubtless an incidental aid to the development of Mr. Altsheler's natural powers as a story-teller for boys and men. But Parkman's vivid, authentic pictures of Indians, Canadians, frontiersmen, the forest itself drew him like a magnet, and he left the way open behind him." (323)

Not many facts are remembered today about the life of Joseph A. Altsheler. If there were ever any personal papers or unpublished manuscripts, they seem to have been lost. (Demaree 22) What is known is that his father and other family members immigrated from Germany and operated a store in Three Springs, Kentucky, not far from Louisville. There Joseph was born in 1862. His mother was descended from a Virginia family that had moved to Kentucky. Joseph married Sarah (Sallie) Boles of Glasgow, Kentucky in 1888. She had been born in 1862 and outlived him by many years. They had a son, Sydney, born in 1892. He never married, and all three are buried in Cave Hill Cemetery in Louisville.

Altsheler studied at Liberty College in Kentucky and Vanderbilt University. In 1885, he joined the staff of the Louisville *Courier-Journal*. In 1892 he joined the New York *World*, becoming the editor of its magazine section. When he couldn't find suitable serials for this magazine, he began to write his own. By my count, he eventually published 48 novels. He also published many short stories in magazines such as *Harpers*, *Cosmopolitan*, *Lippincotts*, *Munsey's World*, and *The Atlantic Monthly*. These stories have never been collected until this book.

Some of Altsheler's novels have a conventional romantic plot ending in marriage, and seem to have been intended for all readers. His most popular novels, however, are adventure stories, primarily for boys. During his last interview with Moore he said he wished to be remembered "as a person who gave young people a reason to read and learn history." Several generations of boys have testified that they learned more history from Altsheler's novels than they did in school. Later writers who have stated that they read and loved Altsheler are Charles Olson, Louis L'Amour, David Herbert Donald, Jack Agueros, AlvinToffler, and Mario Puzo.

Most of Altsheler's novels were published by Appleton. Two were published by Doubleday, one by Lippincott, one by Macmillan, and three by other companies. Appleton promoted Altsheler as "The 20th Century Fenimore Cooper." In December of 1905, he was one of the 170 distinguished guests at Mark Twain's seventieth birthday celebration at Delmonico's in New York. Altsheler's boys' books have been compared to Twain's. When World War I broke out, he and his wife were traveling in Germany, and they had a difficult time getting back to the United States. Altsheler's health (probably his heart) seems to have been damaged by this ordeal, and he was a semi-invalid for the last years of his life. At his death, his estate was valued at over $250,000, attributable to the sale of his novels.

All but two of Altsheler's novels are based on American history, and the great majority have war settings. He set novels during all American wars except the Spanish American. This leads one to wonder that if, like many of his contemporaries, he was not sold on American colonialism. All of the novels except the three in his Great War Series are set in North America, including Canada and Mexico. Altsheler was a careful researcher, and his novels are as historically accurate as he could make them. Historical figures are often characters in the stories. These are famous men such as Lee, Jackson, Houston, Boone, Bowie, and so on.

The main reason for his popularity was probably that he has an excellent prose style. His stories are fast-paced and adventure filled. He depicts an idealized, romantic view of nature. His characters are very well developed. Altsheler had a good sense of humor, so that his novels are thoroughly entertaining.

At the center of all of his serial novels is a brave boy, apparently in his late teens. This boy is often an orphan. If parents are present, they are quickly left at home and play at best a small role in the boy's life. His boys are independent and on their own. There may be a secondary boy hero, a friend of the main hero. While the main hero excels physically, the secondary hero is more of a scholar, destined to be a statesman or newspaper publisher. These boys are usually mentored by an older man who is a very skilled outdoorsman. There is almost always a humorous character in the group, who speaks in a characteristic eccentric manner. None of his main characters is ever killed, or even seriously wounded. They may be exhausted by their trials, but a good night's sleep always restores their healthy bodies.

When one of his characters is captured by Indians, Mexicans, renegades, outlaws, or any foe, it is almost guaranteed that a very violent storm will arise, allowing him to escape in the confusion. Following

Cooper and similar writers, his plots are a series of battles, captures, escapes, and rescues. Nothing really bad ever happens to his captives, other than being taunted by their more wicked captors.

In the July, 1988 issue of *The Filson Club History Quarterly*, Joseph A. Altsheler's niece, Lucy Brent Slater, writes that her uncle's "primary interests" were "reading, writing, and the out-of-doors." (381) Altsheler's love for camping and the wilderness are apparent in his novels, and this is certainly one reason that his books were embraced and endorsed by the Boy Scouts Library in Boy Scout Editions of his novels. In his fiction he depicts the simple pleasures as being the best. Sleeping, eating game cooked on a camp fire, drinking coffee, bathing in clean cold streams and lakes—these are luxuries for his characters.

True to the Boy Scout oath, his characters are "physically strong, mentally awake, and morally straight." They always do their duty to God and country. His heroic boys all love their mothers, but only in the novel *The Young Trailers* does the hero have an actual girlfriend. Of course, there are important female characters in his more adult novels. I am speaking here of his boys' series novels. In his boys' novels women are never wicked; they are just not there. His characters' love of the outdoors and escape from civilization certainly remind the reader of Leatherstocking or Huckleberry Finn.

His group of heroic comrades has not a vice among them, unless drinking coffee is seen as drug addiction. In 1988 *The Young Trailers* was reissued as *Kentucky Frontiersman,* edited by Nathaniel Kenton. Kenton writes that his edition "adds material that the editor believes Altsheler himself would have included had he written today." In this edition Kenton refers once to the frontier having a population of wild women. This is one more mention of sexual vice than Altsheler himself made in all his boys' books.

Altsheler loved history, and his novels are factually accurate. However, it is certainly true that the history he presents is the traditional, heroic, Anglo-Saxon account of British settlers against Native American, Spanish, and Mexican antagonists. The French are also treated sympathetically, especially the missionaries. Whatever the conflict, the American side is always noble and in the right. And the British are also good, unless they are fighting the Americans of course.

In his Civil War novels he presents both sides as heroic. Since Kentucky was a border state, Altsheler knew men who had served on both sides. His Southern heroes are not slave holders, and seem to disapprove of any extension of slavery. Slavery may have been a sensitive topic for Altsheler, because his fiction contains almost no African American characters, and a reader of his novels would find scant mention of the peculiar institution. One would surmise that as a patriotic American, Altsheler was embarrassed by that facet of American history and avoided it as much as possible.

It has been commonly remarked that in American culture Native Americans are often stereotyped as either savage devils or noble savages. James Fenimore Cooper utilized both stereotypes by making some of his tribes noble savages and others savage devils. Much the same could be said of Altsheler's treatment of the American Indian. The American Indian is a major subject in Altsheler's boys' fiction. Sometimes his treatment of Native Americans follows negative stereotypes. I noticed this especially in his Texan Series where the Mexican Indians (Campeachy) are portrayed as cruel and ugly, and the Texas Indians (Comanches and Lipans) are presented as little better.

On the other hand, Altsheler gives a positive portrayal of the Iroquois, and sympathizes with their efforts to preserve their land. Throughout his novels there are many positive portraits of Native Americans. I believe that in his last two series, The French and Indian War and The Great West, his portrait of Native Americans is much more positive. Just as Indian captivity plays a major role in American literature, so it does in Altsheler's fiction. Several of his boy heroes are adopted by Indian tribes, and these tribes are portrayed as brave, just, and honorable.

There is a noticeable element of mysticism and pantheism in some of Altsheler's boys' fiction. This is particularly evident in The Young Trailers Series and the French and Indian War Series. The boy heroes in these series commune with nature, even hearing voices in the winds or rustling leaves. Those who are especially attuned to nature can hear mystical warnings or messages of hope and comfort in the wilderness. In these passages Altsheler asserts that the white man's God and the Great Spirit of the Native Americans are essentially the same.

Although Altsheler's funeral service in Kentucky was conducted by a Methodist minister (Slater 385), he does not seem to have been particularly religious, and his values are largely secular. His praise of missionaries is more for their bravery and honor than for their piety.

An aspect of Altsheler's fiction that would certainly appeal to boys is his emphasis on loyalty and comradeship. One must never betray or abandon a friend. Altsheler celebrates the manly virtues of strength, honesty, courage, and self-reliance. His heroes are always crack shots with excellent eyesight. They are skillful woodsmen. I doubt if any writer has ever portrayed living outdoors to be as cozy and comfortable as he does. The legendary Hemingway hero probably owes a lot to the boys' fiction that was popular when that author was a child. Indeed, in Chapter VII of *The Texan Triumph* a mentor tells the boy hero, "A man ain't ever beat, 'cept when he gives up, an', you don't have to give up." Santiago of *The Old Man and The Sea* couldn't have said it better himself.

In summary, Joseph A. Altsheler was a prolific writer of great gifts. His writing is an important milestone in the development of American juvenile fiction. A writer who was so popular for so long must have had a major impact on popular culture. I believe that his fiction can still be read with pleasure, and that he deserves to be much more widely known that he is today.

* * * * *

Most of this article appeared originally in "The Serial Fiction of Joseph A. Altsheler," *Dime Novel Round-Up*, 74 (October, 2005), 176-183.

Works Cited

Demaree,Ona Belle. "Joseph Altsheler: His Contribution to American Fiction for Boys," Masters Thesis, University of Louisville, 1938.

Moore, Anne (sometimes written Annie) Carroll. *My Roads To Childhood: Views and Reviews of Children's Books*, The Horn Book, Boston, 1961

——. *The Three Owls*, The Macmillian Company, New York, 1925.

Slater, Lucy Bent. "Kentucky's Most Prolific Author. *The Filson Club History Quarterly* 62 (July 1988): 380-388.

Altsheler's Serial Novels

The Young Trailers Series
(Set on the frontier during the American Revolution. His best known series, and perhaps his best work.)
- *The Young Trailers* (1907)
- *The Forest Runners* (1908)
- *The Keepers of the Trail* (1916)
- *The Eyes of the Woods* (1917)
- *The Free Rangers* (1909)
- *The Riflemen of the Ohio* (1910
- *The Scouts of the Valley* (1912)
- *The Border Watch* (1912)

The Civil War Series
(The main characters in these novels are descendants of the major characters in The Young Trailers Series. They are Kentucky natives in both series.)
- *The Guns of Bull Run* (1914)
- *The Guns of Shiloh* (1914)
- *The Scouts of Stonewall* (1914)
- *The Sword of Antietam* (1914)
- *The Star of Gettysburg* (1915)
- *The Rock of Chickamauga* (1915)
- *The Shades of the Wilderness* (1916)
- *The Tree of Appomattox* (1916)

The Texan Series
- *The Texan Star* (1912)
- *The Texan Scouts* (1913)
- *The Texas Triumph* (1913)

The Great War Series
- *The Guns of Europe* (1915)
- *The Forest of Swords* (1915)
- *The Hosts of the Air* (1915)

The French and Indian War Series
- *The Lords of the Wild* (1919)
- *The Hunters of the Hills* (1916)
- *The Shadow of the North* (1917)
- *The Sun of Quebec* (1919)
- *The Rulers of the Lakes* (1917)
- *The Masters of the Peaks* (1918)

The Great West Series (Apparently unfinished)
- *The Great Sioux Trail* (1918)
- *The Lost Hunters* (1918)

Other Boys' Novels
- *The Rainbow of Gold* (1896)
- *The Hidden Mine* (1896) This is a sequel to *Rainbow.*
- *The Last of the Chiefs* (1909)
- *The Horsemen of the Plains* (1910)
- *The Quest of the Four* (1911)
- *Apache Gold* (1913)

Novels with an adult hero and a love story ending in marriage
- *A Soldier of Manhattan* (1897) Criticized by Henry James for its lack of historical authenticity.
- *The Sun of Saratoga* (1897) Reissued as late as 1971 as a paperback romance novel.
- *A Herald of the West* (1898)
- *In Circling Camps* (1898)
- *In Hostile Red* (1900)
- *The Last Rebel* (1900)
- *The Wilderness Road* (1901)
- *My Captive* (1902)
- *Before the Dawn* (1903)
- *Guthrie of the Times* (1904)
- *The Candidate* (1905)
- *The Recovery* (1909)

After 1909, Altsheler published only boys' fiction.

Introduction, Part 2

The Short Stories of Joseph A. Altsheler

ROBERT M. MCILVAINE

As a fiction writer, Joseph A. Altsheler had a dual personality. On the one hand, he wrote vigorous, exciting tales of adventure. These novels and short stories constitute by far his best work, and can still be read with enjoyment today. On the other hand, he wrote sentimental romantic melodramas where an innocent girl is rescued from a terrible fate by a chivalrous young man. Inevitably, the two marry and live happily ever after. Similarly, he wrote a series of narratives staring noble, idealistic politicians, knights in shining armor who are richly rewarded for their virtue. While these stories and novels may have had some interest in Altsheler's day, they are not at all to modern taste. Altsheler's adventure stories seem to have been written by another person, and they are all he wrote for the last decade of his life.

During the first half of the Twentieth Century, Altsheler's serial novels for boys were very popular. As a writer primarily for adolescent or pre-adolescent boys, his most popular works feature male characters. "At the Twelfth Hour" is the only story in this collection that features a female character, and she is a sort of earth mother figure. Altsheler could write well of mother-son relationships, but he was totally discombobulated by romantic relationships. In this he was a quintessential Victorian.

"At the Twelfth Hour" and "After the Battle" are Altsheler's best short stories. Over the last hundred years they have been included in several anthologies of short stories or Civil War fiction. However, they are certainly not readily available to the reader. To my knowledge, none of the other stories in this collection has ever been reprinted.

Although Altsheler, like Stephen Crane, was too young to have served in the Civil War, like Crane he had heard many stories of the war told by veterans of that conflict. In their mixture of realism and impressionism, "At the Twelfth Hour" and "After the Battle" are strongly suggestive of the best Civil War stories of Crane or Ambrose Bierce. Like Bierce, Altsheler relies a great deal on coincidence in his Civil War stories, but this was typical of the stories of the time in which surprise endings were conventional.

As has been stated, "At the Twelfth Hour" is very unusual for Altsheler because its main character is a strong woman. A modern touch in the story is the ambiguity about whether the mother has actually found her wounded youngest son, or whether she is doing for another boy what she wishes had been done for her son when he was wounded and dying. She rescues the young soldier because he reminds her of her own son; the clear implication is that all the soldiers in the Civil War are sons of America. A common theme in Altsheler's Civil War fiction is reconciliation between the North and the South.

Because he was a native of the border state of Kentucky, this reconciliation theme may have had special significance for him. As a boy growing up in Kentucky, he had heard stories from both Confederate and Union veterans. "After the Battle" is another strong story of reconciliation between North and South, personified by reconciliation between representatives of two feuding Kentucky families.

While "The Break of Day" and "Guard No. 10" are not as dramatic as "At the Twelfth Hour" and "After the Battle," they are still very readable stories that emphasize the kinship between North and South. "The Retreat of the Ten," set immediately after the Civil War, dramatizes the return to Union allegiance by former Confederate soldiers.

"The Escape" is another story of feuding Kentucky families, again with a healing conclusion similar to "After the Battle."

"In Sheep's Clothing" is another good story, again with a frontier setting reminiscent of The Young Trailers series. The main villain in The Young Trailers books is the renegade Braxton Wyatt. Unlike Wyatt, the renegade in this story is redeemed from his evil way of life. A weakness of this story is the very negative stereotyping of the Native American characters. In his best fiction, Altsheler gives a much more positive portrayal of the Native American tribes.

The other Altsheler stories that I have found are much weaker. "The Wedding Guest" and "The Pirate and the Maid" are preposterous poppycock. Seven of the stories became chapters in his novel *The Candidate*, and can be read there by any who might be interested. This has never been a popular novel, however. Two other stories seem to have been written for *The Candidate* or another of his political novels, but were omitted from publication.

I believe that "At the Twelfth Hour" is Altsheler's masterpiece, worthy of comparison with the best Civil War fiction of Crane and Bierce. The other stories included in this collection are also much too good to be forgotten.

I have chosen to include the autobiographical article "What the Homecomers Saw" because of what it reveals about the attitudes of the author, both his strong points and what would be seen today as his weaknesses. I also think that it is worthwhile because information about Altsheler is quite scarce.

Altsheler's Short Stories

Civil War Stories

These are, by far, his best short stories. Their common theme is reconciliation of the North and South.

- "After the Battle," *Lippincott's*, 61 (1898) 368-88
- At the Twelfth Hour: A Tale of a Battle," *Atlantic Monthly*, 82 (October, 1898), 541-58.

The two stories listed above are his best, and have occasionally been included in anthologies of American short stories or Civil War short stories.

- "The Break of Day," *Munsey's*, 16 (1895), 579-82,
- "Guard No. 10," *Munsey's*, 19 (1898), 952-54.
- "The Retreat of the Ten," *Cosmopolitan*, 38 (November 4, 1904), 33-42.

Adventure Stories
- "The Escape," *Harper's Weekly*, 47 (June 6, 1903), 940-42.
- "The Island Chute," *Harper's Weekly*, 47 (December 12, 1903), 11.
- "The Lone Huntsman," *Lippincott's*, 82 (October 1908), 496-503.
- "In Sheep's Clothing," *The American Boy*, (February 1919), 20, 32.

Melodramatic Love Stories
- "The Wedding Guest," *Harper's Monthly Magazine*, 107 (October 1903), 668-74.
- "The Pirate and the Maid," *The Red Book Magazine*, (1906), 604-12.

Stories that became chapters in his novel *The Candidate* (1905)
- "His Greatest Speech," *Harper's Monthly Magazine*, 105 (June 1902), 131-38.
- "Jimmy Grayson's Spell," *Harper's Weekly*, 47 (August 15, 1903), 1344-48.
- "The Third Degree," *Harper's Weekly*, 47 (August 22 , 1903), 1380-4.
- The Dead City," *Harper's Weekly*, 47 (October 24, 1903), 1712-6.
- "The Spellbinder," *Harper's Weekly*, 48 (October 29, 1904), 1666-7.

Other Political Stories
- "Dawn in the Desert," *Harper's Weekly*, 47 (July 25 and August 1, 1903), 1236-9, 1272-4. This story was omitted from *The Candidate*, but concerns the same characters and events.
- "The Changing Order," *The Monthly Story Blue Book Magazine*, IV, No. 3 (January 1907), 433-87. The introduction in the magazine calls this a novel.

- "The Governor's Choice," *Lippincott's*, 70 (August 1902), 165-76. This story could have been written as part of the novel *Guthrie of the Times* (1904) as Guthrie is a major character, as he is in *The Recovery* (1909). However, it is not included in either novel.

Section I

Civil War Stories

Chapter 1

At the Twelfth Hour: A Tale of a Battle

There was no pause in the clamor outside, which rose sometime to a higher key, and then sank back to its level, like the rush of a storm. Every log and plank in the little house would tremble as if it were so much human flesh and blood, when a crash louder than the rest betokened the sudden discharge of all the guns in some battery. The loose windows rattled in their wooden frames alike before the roar of the artillery and the shriller note of the rifles, which clattered and buzzed without ceasing, and seemed to boast a sting sharper and more deadly than that of their comrades the big guns. Whiffs of smoke, like the scud blown about by the winds at sea, would pass before the windows and float off into the forest. Sometimes a yellow light, that wavered like heat-lightning, would shine through the glass and quiver for a moment or two across the wooden floor. In the east there was a haze, a mottled blur of red and yellow and blue, and whether the crash of the artillery rose or sank, whether the clatter of the rifles was louder or weaker, there came always the unbroken din of two hundred thousand men foot to foot in battle,—a shuffling, moaning noise, a shriek, then a roar.

The widow moved the table and its dim candle nearer the window, not that she might see better outside, but there she could have a stronger light on her sewing, which was important and must be finished. The blaze of the battle flared in at the window more than once, and flickered across her face, revealing the strong , harsh features, and the hundreds of fine wrinkles that crossed one another in countless mazes, and clustered under her eyes and around the corners of her mouth. She was not a handsome woman, nor had ever been, even on her bridal morning, but she was still tall and muscular, her figure clothed in a poor print dress,— one who had endured much, and could endure more. As she bent over humble sewing the dim light of the candle was reflected in hopeless eyes.

The battle rolled a little nearer from the east, and the flashes of its light grew more frequent. The trembling of the house never ceased. On the hearth-stone some tiny half-dead embers danced about under the incessant rocking, like popping grains of corn, and the windows in their frames droned out their steady rattle.

But the widow paid no heed, going on with her sewing. The battle was nothing to her. She did not care who won; she would not go out of her house to see. If men were such barbarians and brutes as to murder one another for they knew not what, then let them. The more human flesh and blood the war devoured, the greater its appetite grew; for upon such food it fattened and prospered. Her three sons had gone to the man-eater, gulped down, one, two, three, in the order of their age: first the eldest, then the second, and then her youngest, her best beloved. She had thought that he, at least, who would not be a man for years, might be left to her; but the news had come from Shiloh, in a meager letter written by a comrade; that he had fallen there, mortally wounded, and the enemy who kept the field had buried him, perhaps.

She had the letter yet, but she never looked at it. There was no need, when she knew every line, every word, every letter, and just how they looked and stood on the page. The two older sons, like so many of the men of those wild hill regions, had been worthless,—drinkers of whiskey, tellers of lies, squalid loafers blinking at the sun; but the third, the boy, had been different, and she had expected him to become a man such as a woman could admire, a man upon whom a woman could depend,— that is, one stronger than herself, and as good. He had been both son and daughter to her, for in that way a mother looks upon the youngest or only son when he has no sister; but fair hair and blue eyes and a girl face had not prevented him from following the others, and now she knew not even where his bones lay, save that the mould of a wide and desolate battle-field inclosed them, and, in some place, hid them.

This woman did not cry; no tears came from her eyes when the news of the boy's death was brought to her, and none came now, when she still saw him, fair-haired and white-faced, lying out there under the sky. She had merely become harsher and harder, and, never much given to speech, she spoke less than before.

The battle rolled yet a little nearer from the east, and the complaining windows rattled more loudly. Above the thud of the cannon and the unbroken crash of the rifles she could hear now the shouting of many men, a guttural tumult which brought to mind the roar and shriek of wild animals in combat. The coming of the twilight did not seem to diminish their ferocity, and, repeating her old formula, she said, "Let them fight on through the night, if it pleases them."

The earth rumbled and rocked beneath a mighty discharge of artillery, the old house shook, and the heap of coals rolled down and scattered over the hearth. She walked from the window and put them carefully in place with an iron shovel. Thrown back together they sent up little spears of flame, which cast a flickering light over the desolate room,— the bare wooden floor, the rough log walls spotted with a few old newspaper prints, the two pine tables, the cane-bottomed chairs, the home-made wooden stool, the iron kettle in one corner and the tin pans beside it, the low bed covered with a brown counterpane in another corner,—a room that suited the mind and the temper of the woman who owned it and lived in it.

The battle crept still closer; the departed sun, the twilight deepening into night, had no effect on the fury of the combatants. Gun answered gun, and the rifles hurled opposing showers of lead. The difference in the two notes of the battle, the sullen, bass thunder of the cannon with its curious trembling cadence, and the sharper, shriller crash of the small arms, like the wrath of little people, became clearer, more distinct. Over both, in irregular waves, swelled the shouting; the wild and piercing "rebel yell" and the hoarse Yankee cheer contending and mingling and rolling back and forth in a manner that would tell nothing to a listener save that men were in mortal combat.

She heard a shrieking noise, like the scream of a man, but far louder; a long trail of light appeared in the sky, curving and arching like a rainbow until it touched the earth, when it disappeared in one grand explosion, throwing red, blue, green and yellow lights into the air, as if a little volcano had burst. She almost fancied she could hear pieces of the shell whizzing through the air, though it was only fancy; but she knew that the earth where it struck had been torn up, and the dead were scattered about like its own pieces. Up went another, and another, and the air was filled with them, shining and shrieking as if in delight because they gave the finish and crowning touch to the battle. She watched them with a certain pleasure as they curved so beautifully, and gave herself praise when she

timed to the second the moment of striking the earth. Soon the air was
filled with a shower of curving lights, and then they ceased for a while.

Still the dim battle raged in the darkness. But presently a light flared
up again and did not disappear. It burned with a steady red and blue
flame that indicated something more than the flashing of cannon and
rifles, and, looking through a window-pane, the widow saw the cause.
The forest was on fire, the exploding gun powder having served as a
torch; the blaze ran high above the trees, adding a new rush and roar to
the thunder and sweep of the battle. But she was calm; for the forest did
not come near enough to place her house in danger of the fire, and there
was no reason why she need disturb herself. She blew out the candle,
carefully put away in the cupboard the piece remaining,—economy being
both a virtue and a necessity with her,—and returned to her seat by the
window, now lighted only by the blaze of the battle and the burning
trees. The light from the flaming forest grew stronger, and flared through
the window all the way across the room. When the flash of the guns
joined it, the glare was so vivid that the widow was compelled to shield
her eyes with her hand; she would have closed the shutter of the window
and relighted the candle, had there been a shutter to close. Clouds of
smoke—some light, white, and innocent-looking, others heavy and black—
floated past the window. Such clouds were needed, she thought, to veil
the horrors of the slaughter-yard outside. She looked at the little tin clock
on the mantel, ticking placidly away, and saw that it was a quarter to ten.
She would have gone to bed, but one could not sleep with all that noise
outside and so near. She thought it wise to take her old seat by the
window and watch the flames from the forest, because sparks driven by
the wind might fall on her house and set it on fire. There were two
buckets filled with water in the little lean-to that served as a kitchen, and
she set them in a place that would be handy in case the dangerous sparks
came.

But she did not think the water would be needed, since the wind,
though light, was blowing the fire from her. This was indicated clearly
by the streams of flame, red in the center, blue and white at the edges,
which leaned eastward. The fire had gathered full volume now, and gave
her a gorgeous spectacle, the flames leaping far above the trees, where
they united into cones and pyramids, flashing with many colors and sending
forth millions of sparks, which curved up, and then fell like showers of
fireflies. Under this flaming cloud, the cannon spouted and the rifles
flashed with as much steadiness and vigor as ever. It seemed to be a vast

panoramic effect in fire planned for her alone, after the fashion of the Roman emperors, of whom she had never heard.

By the light of the fire and the battle she saw, for the first time, some figures struggling in the chaos of flame and smoke. Human beings she knew them to be, though they looked but little like it, being mere writhing black lines in a whirl of red fire and blue smoke. It was a living picture, to her, of the infernal regions, in which she was a firm believer; those ghastly shapes straining and fighting among the eternal flames. She felt a little sympathy for the many—mostly boys like her own boy who had fallen at Shiloh—who were about to pass through the flames of this world into the flames of the next; for she had been taught that only one out of a hundred could be saved, and she never doubted it. If she felt doubt at all, it was about the deserts of the hundredth man.

The thunder of the cannon sank presently to a mutter and a growl, the rifles ceased entirely, and the sudden drop in the noise of the battle caused the fire's roar to be heard above it like a tempest. She could still see the black figures, so many jumping-jacks, through the veil of flame and smoke; but they were now a confused and struggling heap without plan or order; they had drawn apart in two lines, and for two or three minutes remained motionless, save for a few figures which strutted up and down and waved what looked through the fiery mist like little sticks, but which she knew to be long swords. She knew enough more to guess that one line was about to charge the other, or more likely, both would charge at the same time, and the sinking of the battle was but a pause to gather strength for a supreme effort.

She was interested, and her interest increased when she saw the opposing lines swing forward a little, as if making ready for the shock. The sudden ebb of the firing had made all other noises curiously distinct. The ticking of the little clock on the mantel became a steady drumbeat. She even fancied that she could hear the commands given to the two lines of puny black figures, but she knew it was only fancy.

This silence, so heavy that it oppressed her, after all she had heard, was broken by the discharge of hidden batteries, so many great guns at once that the widow sprang up from her chair; she thought at first that the house was falling about her, and she clapped her hands to her ears to shut out the penetrating crash, which was succeeded by the fierce, unbroken shrieking of the small arms. The clouds of smoke at once thickened and darkened, but she could see through it the two lines, now dim gray images of men, rushing upon each other. She watched with eager, intent eyes. The whirling smoke would hide parts of one line for a moment, leaving it a series of disconnected fragments; then would drift away, revealing the unbroken ranks again. She could hear the ticking of the clock no longer, for the pounding of the guns was so terrific now that continuous thunder roared in her ears, inside her head, and seemed not to come from anything without. A window-pane broke under the impact of so much sound, and the fragments of glass rattled on the floor, but she did not take her eyes from the battle.

Over the heads of the rushing lines the smoke formed in a cloud so thick, so black, so threatening, and so low that it inclosed them, like a roof. The old likeness came back to the widow. It is the roof of hell, she said to herself; these walls and pillars of flame are its sides, and the men who fight in there, hemmed in by fire, are the damned, condemned to fight so forever.

On they rushed, some of the dim gray figures seeming to dance above the earth in the flames, like the imps they were, and the two lines met midway. She thought she could hear the smash of wave on wave above the red roar of the guns, and figures shot into the air as if hurled up by the meeting of tremendous and equal forces. A long cry, a yell, a shriek, and a wail, which could come only from human throats, thousands of them together, swelled again above everything else,—above the roar of the fire, above the crash of the rifles, above the thunder of the cannon.

In spite of her stoicism the watcher quivered a little and turned her eyes away from the window, but she turned them back again. The cry sank to a quaver, then rose again to a scream; and thus it sank and rose, as the battle surged from side to side in the flaming pit. She thought she could hear the clash of arms, bayonet on bayonet, sword on sword, and all the sounds of war became confused and mingled, like the two lines of men which had rushed so fiercely together. There were no longer two lines,—not even one line,—but a medley; struggling heaps, red whirlpools which threw out their dead and whirled on, grinding up the living like grain in a hopper. The soldiers fought into the very center of the pit, and the shifting red curtain of flame between gave them strange shapes, enlarging some, belittling others, and then blending all into a blurred mass, a huddle of men without form or number.

Fantastic and horrible, the scene appealed strongly to the widow's hard religious sense. She could no longer doubt that the red chaos upon which she was looking was a picture of life from the regions of eternal torture, reserved for the damned, reproduced on earth for the benefit of men. It was, then, with a feeling of increased interest that she watched the battle as it blazed and shrieked to and fro. The thunder of the cannon and the crash of the rifles were still as steady as the rush of a tempest, and the wild shouting of the men now rose above the din, then was crushed out by it, only to be heard again, fiercer and shriller than before.

The great clouds which lowered over the pit grew blacker and bigger, and rolled away in somber waves on every side. Their vanguard reached even to her house and passed over it. The loathsome smell of burnt gunpowder and raw and roasted human flesh came in at the broken window. She stuffed a quilt into the open space, until neither smoke nor smell could enter; but some of the droppings of the black cloud, little balls and curls of smoke, came down the chimney and floated about the room, to remind the woman that the whirlwind of the battle whirled widely enough to draw her in, too. Her throat felt hot and scaly, and she took a gourd of water from one of the buckets and drank it. It was cool to the throat, and as smooth as oil. How some of these men lying out there, helpless on the ground, longed for water, cold water! How her own boy, doubtless, had longed for it, as he lay on the field at Shiloh waiting for the death that came! A feeling of pity, a strong feeling, swelled up in her soul. She walked again across the room and looked at the little tin clock on the mantel. Ten forty-five! It was time for the battle to close; it had been time long ago.

Then she went back as usual to the window, and she noticed at once that the roar and blaze of the battle were sinking. The thunder of the guns was not continuous, and the intervals increased in number and became longer. The fire of the rifles was broken into crackling showers, and spots of gray or white, where the air was breaking through, appeared in the wall of flame. The black roof of smoke lifted a little, and seemed to be losing length and breadth as the wind swept off cloudy patches and carried them away. The fire in the forest was dying, and she ceased to hear the rush of the flames from tree to tree. Once the human shout or shriek—she could not tell which—came to her ear, but she heard it no more just then. The men, more distinct now as the veil of flame thinned away or rose in vapor, still struggled, but with less ferocity. The groups were breaking up, and the two lines shrank apart, each seeming to abandon the ground for which it had fought.

It was nearly eleven o'clock, and the moon, able for the first time to send its beams through the battle-smoke, was beginning to cast a silvery radiance over the field. The flames sank fast. The fire in the forest burnt out. The great cloud of smoke broke up into many little clouds which drifted away westward before the wind. The showers of sparks ceased, and the bits of charred wood no longer fell. A fine cloud of ashes blown through the air began to form a film over the window-panes.

The battle died like the eruption of a volcano, which shoots up with all its strength, and then sinks from exhaustion. The human figures melted away, and the last was gone, though the widow knew that many must be lying in the ravines and on the hillsides beyond her view. There were four cannon-shots at irregular intervals, the fourth a long time after the third, a volley or two from the rifles, a pop-pop or two, and the firing was over. Some feeble flames from grass or bush still spurted up, but they fought in a lost cause, for the silver radiance of the moon grew, and they paled and sank back before it.

The ticking of the clock made the cessation of noise outside more noticeable. She opened the window, and the air that came in was strong with a fleshy smell. But so much smoke had come down the chimney, and the room was so close, that she kept the window open and let the air seek every corner. Outside, the unburnt trees were swaying in the west wind, but there was no other noise. The battlefield, unlighted by the fire of cannon and rifles, had become invisible; but she knew that many men were lying there, and the wind sobbing through the burnt and unburnt forest was their dead march.

Fine ashes, borne by the wind from the burnt forest, still fell; some came in at the open window, and fell in a faint whitish powder on the floor. The widow took her wisp broom and brushed the ashes carefully into the fire; but she did not close the window, for the fresh air which blew in had a tonic strength, though there was still about it some of that strange odor, the breath of slaughter.

She resolved to watch the field a little longer, and then she would go to bed; she had wasted enough time watching the struggles of lost souls. The light of the moon was beginning to wane, and the trees and hills were growing more shadowy; their silver gray was changing to black, the somber hue borrowed from the skies above them. Flecks of fire like smouldering coals gleamed through the darkness, showing where a tree-trunk or a bush still burned in the wake of the battle or the fire. The wind rose again, and these tiny patches of flame blazed before it more brightly for a time, and then went out. But the wind moaned more loudly as it blew among the burned tree-trunks and the dead branches. Some trees, eaten through by the fire, fell, and the night, so still otherwise, echoed with the sound.

All the lights from the fire went out, but others took their place. She could see them far apart, but twinkling like little stars fallen to earth; probably the lanterns, she thought, of surgeons and soldiers come to look for those whose wounds were not mortal. Why not let them lie there and pay the price of their own folly? They had gone into the battle knowing its risks, and they should not seek to shun them. She would go to bed, and she put up her hand to pull down the window. She heard a prolonged cry, a wail and a sob; distant, perhaps, and feeble, but telling of pain and fear.

It came direct from the battlefield. She would have dismissed the sound, as she had dismissed all other signs of the battle, but it came again and was more penetrating. She thought that she had no fancy, no imagination, and that the battle had passed leaving her mind untouched, but the cry lingered. It rose for the third time, louder, fuller, more piercing than before, and the air ached with it. She was sure now that it was many voices in one, all groaning in their agony, and their groans uniting in a single lament, which rose above that of the wind and filled all of the air with its wailing. She tried again to crush down her thoughts, and to hide the scenes that she saw with her mind, and not with her eyes; but her will refused to obey her, and yielded readily to imagination, which, held back so long, took possession of its kingdom with despotic power. Her face and hands became cold and wet at the sights and scenes that her fancy made her hear and see. It was easy to turn this field into the field of Shiloh, and her ready imagination, laughing at her will, did it for her. In that other battle her boy was lying at the foot of a hillock, his white face growing whiter, turned up to the stars; the dead lay around him, and there was no sound but his groans.

But the cry of anguish from the field reached her there; fainter, more muffled, but not to be mistaken. Whether it came through the glass or how else, she knew not, but she heard it,—a cry to her, a cry that would reach her even in bed and would not let her sleep. It was as if her own son had been crying to her for help, for water. She threw up the window again, and looked toward the battlefield. The air was filled with the cries of the wounded like the chorus of the lost, but of the field itself she could see nothing. The night had darkened fast, and the ground on which the men had fought was clothed in a ghostly vapor. The burnt trees were but a faint tracery of black, and the wind had ceased, leaving the night, hot, close, and breathless. The fine ashes from the fire no longer fell, and the air was free from them, but was thick and heavy, and the repellent smell of human flesh lingered. It was a terrible night for the wounded. They would lie on the ground in the close heat and gasp for air, which would be like fire to their lungs.

The little clock struck midnight with a loud, emphatic tang, each stroke echoing and reminding her that it was time to go.

The two buckets filled with water, which she had brought to save her house from fire, still stood by the window. She put the drinking-gourd into one of them, lifted both, and passed out of the house. She was a strong woman, and she did not stagger beneath the weight of the water. This, she knew, was what they would want most; for in all that she had ever heard of battlefields the cry for water was loudest. Yet all her pity in that moment was for one,—not one of those who lay there, but her own boy on that other battlefield. She saw only him, only his face; like a girl's it had looked to her, with its youthful flush and the fair hair around it. It was he, not the others, who was taking her out on the field, and she walked on with straight, strong steps, because he led her.

The mists and vapors seemed to drift away as she approached the battlefield, and the trees, holding out their burnt arms, rose distinct and clear from the darkness. The cries of the wounded increased, and were no longer a steady volume like the moaning of the wind; but she could distinguish in the tumult articulate sounds, even words, and they were always the same,—the cry for water rising above all others, just as she had been told. She reached the ground over which the fire had swept. Some clusters of sparks, invisible from the window, lingered yet in the clefts of roots and rocks, and glimmered like marsh lights.

The strange repellent odor that reminded her of the drippings of a slaughter-house attacked her with renewed strength. She turned a little sick, but she conquered her faintness and went on. Wisps of smoke were still drifting about, and she stumbled on something and nearly fell; but she saved the precious water, and saw that her foot had struck against a cannon-ball, which lay there, half buried in the earth, spent, after its mission. To her eyes the earth upon it was the color of blood, and giving it a look of repulsion she passed on. She saw two or three rifles upon the ground, abandoned by their owners; and here was a broken sword, and there a knapsack, still full, which some soldier had thrown away. Under the half-burned trunk of a tree was something dark and shapeless, and charred like the tree; but she knew what it was, and after the first glance kept her head turned away. She passed more like it, but all were motion-less, for the fire had spared nothing over which it had gone.

The smell of roasted flesh was strong here, but the silence appalled her. All the cries came from the further part of the field, and around her no voice was raised. The figures, half hidden in the dark, did not stir. The trees waved their burnt arms, and gave forth a dry, parched sound when a whiff of wind struck them, like the rustle of a field of dead broom sedge.

She crossed the strip over which the fire had swept and burned out everything living, and entered the red battlefield beyond. It was lighter here, for there were fewer trees and the moon had cleared somewhat. She saw many figures of men; some motionless as they had been in the burnt woods; others twisting and distorting themselves like spiders on a pin; and still others half sitting or leaning against a stone or a stump, and trying to bind up their own wounds. The cries were a medley, chiefly groans and shrieks, but sometimes laughter, and twice a song. She had never seen ground so torn, for here the battle had trod to and fro in all its strength and ferocity. Three or four trees, cut down by cannon-balls, had fallen together, their boughs interlaced, and a hole in the earth showed where a huge shell had burst. Some sharp pieces of the exploding iron had been driven into a neighboring tree, and a little further on a patch of bushes had been mowed down like grass in a hayfield.

A man, shot in the legs, who had propped himself against a rock, saw the water that she carried, and cried to her to come to him with it. He damned her from a full vocabulary because she did not make enough haste, and when she came tried to snatch the gourd from her hand. But with her stronger hand she pushed his away, and made him drink while she held the gourd. He was young, but it did not seem strange to her to hear such volleys of profanity from one who had the splendor of youth, for her older sons had been of his kind. She left him cursing her because she did not give him more water, and went on; for the face of her boy was still leading her, and the one she left was not like his.

The field extended further than she could see, but all around her was the lament of after-the-battle. Lights trembled or glimmered over the field; the surgeons and soldiers holding them were seeking the wounded, and she saw that some wore the blue and others the gray. Such a shambles as this was the only place in which they could meet like brethren, and here they passed each other without comment; nor did they notice her, save one, an old man with the shining tools of a surgeon in his hand, who gave her an approving nod.

She heard a moan which seemed to come from a little clump of bushes spared by the cannon-balls. A man,—a boy, rather,—with the animal instinct, had crawled in there that he might die unseen. He was in delirium with fever, and cried for his mother. The widow's heart was touched more deeply than before, for it was to such as he that her boy's face was leading her. She took him from out the bushes, stanched his wounds, and gave him of the cold water to drink. The fever abated, and his delirious talk sank to a mere mutter, while she stood and watched until one of the wagons gathering up the wounded came by; then she helped put him in, and passed on with the water to the others. She was eager to help; it was true pity, not a mere sense of duty, for she was now among the boys, the slender lads of eighteen and seventeen and sixteen; and very many of them there were, too, and she knew that her own boy had called her to help these. They lay thick upon the ground,—children they seemed to her; yet this war had such in scores of thousands, who went from the country schoolhouses to the battlefield.

Most of them were dead; sometimes they lay in long rows, as if they had been made ready for the grave; sometimes they lay in a heap, their bodies crossing; and here and there lay one who had found death alone. But amid the dead were a few living, and the widow's hands grew tenderer and more gentle as she raised their heads and let them drink. The water in her buckets was three fourths gone, and she was very careful of it now, for a little might mean a life.

The vapors still hung over the field, and the thick, clammy air was often death to the wounded who could not breathe it. The widow wished more than once for a little of the water, herself, but there were others who needed it far more, and she went on with her work among the boys. She thought often, as she looked at the white young faces around her, of that slaughter of the innocents of which the Bible told, and it seemed to her that this was as wicked and fruitless as that.

The lights were growing fewer, and the carts with the wounded rumbled past her less often; the cries, a volume of sound before, became solitary moans. The darkness, cut here and there by the vapors, hid most of the field, and she was forced to search closely to tell the living from the dead. She was tired, weary in bone and sinew, but the face of her boy led her on, and, while any of the living remained there, she would seek. She stumbled once, in the darkness, on a dead body, and springing back with a shudder when she felt the yielding flesh under feet, walked on into a little hollow.

She heard a boy groan,—very feebly, but still she could not mistake the sound for any of the fancied noises of the battlefield; and then the same faint voice calling his mother. She had heard other boys, on that night, calling for their mothers, but there was a new tone in this cry. She trembled and stood quite still, listening for the groan, which came again, feebler than before. It was so faint that she could not tell from what point it came, and all the shadows seemed to have gathered in the hollow. If she had only a light! She saw one of the lanterns glimmering far off in the field, but even if she obtained it she might not be able to find the place again. She advanced into the hollow, bending down low and searching the thick weeds and tangled bushes with her eyes. One of the buckets she had left behind; the other yet contained a gourd full of water, and she preserved it as if it were so much gold, now more jealously than ever.

She saw nothing. The place was larger than she had thought, and was thick with vines and weeds and heaped-up stones. She stumbled twice and fell upon her knees, but each time she held the water so well that not a drop was spilled. She stood erect again, listening, but hearing nothing. She called aloud, saying that help was there, but no answer came. Her heart was beating violently, but she neither wept nor cried aloud, for she was a woman of strength, and had always been of few words and less show.

Where she stood was the lowest point of the battlefield, and was on its outer edge. It was likewise the darkest spot, and the remainder of it seemed to curve before and above her in a great dusky amphitheater, broken faintly by a few points of light where the lantern burned. She saw the formless bulk of a single cart moving slowly. In a little while the field would be abandoned to her and the dead.

She turned and continued the search, feeling her way through the mass of vegetation, and listening for the guiding groan. Again she stopped, and her heart was in the grip of fear lest she should not find him. She bent her ear close to the ground, and then she heard a cry so faint that it was but a sigh. She pushed her way through some bushes, and there he lay, his back against a rock, his white girlish face with its circle of fair hair turned up to the sky. The eyes were closed, and the chest seemed not to move. A great clot of blood hung upon his left shoulder and made a red gleam against the cloth of his coat.

Let it be said again that she was not a woman who showed her emotions, though at that first glance her face perhaps turned as white as his. She set the bucket down, knelt at his side, and, putting her face close to his, found that he was not dead, for she felt his breath upon her lips. She raised the head a little, and a sigh of pain, scarcely to be heard, escaped him. She poured some of the water, every drop more precious now than ever, into the gourd, and moistened his lips, which burned with fever. Then she raised his head higher and dropped a little into his mouth. He sighed again, and his eyelids quivered and were lifted until a faint trace of the blue beneath appeared; then they closed. But she poured water into his mouth and down his throat a second time, and she could feel that pulse and breathing were stronger.

The blood clotted and caked over his wound, but with wisdom she let it alone, knowing that there was no better bandage to stop the flow. She wet his hands and face with water and gave him more to drink, and saw a trace of color appear in his cheeks. His eyes opened partly two or three times, and he talked, but not of anything she knew, speaking in confused words of other battlefields and long marches; and before a sentence or its sense was finished another would be begun. She wanted no help; she looked around in jealousy lest another should come, and saw how small was the chance of it. The last cart had disappeared from the field, so far as she could see; she could count but four lights, and they were far off. In that part of the field, she, the living, was alone with the dead and the boy who hung between life and death.

Never had she felt herself more strong of body and mind, more full of resource; never had she felt herself more ready of head and hand. She gave him the last of the water, and saw the spot of color in his cheek, which was not of fever, grow. Then she lifted him in her arms, and began to walk with her burden across the battlefield. She looked at the wound, and seeing no fresh blood knew that she had not strained it open in lifting. With that she was satisfied, and she went on with careful step.

She felt her way through the roughness of the hollow, where the bushes and the weeds clung to her dress and her feet and tried to trip her; but she thrust them all aside and went on toward the house. She passed out of the hollow, and into the space which had received the full sweep of the cannon-balls and bullets.

The field was clothed in vapors which floated around her like little clouds. The white faces of the dead looked up at her, and she seemed to be going between rows of them on either side.

She walked on with sure and steady step, not feeling the weight in her arms and against her shoulder, unmoved by the ghastly heaps and the dead faces. She reached the burnt ground, where the little patches of fire that she had seen as she passed the other way had ceased to burn, but the smoke was still rising and the ground was yet warm. She feared that the smoke would get into his throat and choke down the little life that was left. So she ran, and the burnt arms of the trees seemed to wave at her and to jeer her, as if they knew she would be too late. She stumbled a little, but recovered herself. The boy stirred and groaned. She was in dread lest the rough jolt had started his wound, but her hand could not feel the warmth of fresh blood, and, reassured, she hastened through the burnt strip and toward home.

The house was silent and dark; apparently, no one had noticed the log cabin, its secluded position and the clump of woods perhaps hiding it from men whose attention had been devoted solely to the battle. She pushed open the door, and entered with her helpless burden. Some coals still glowed on the hearth, and threw out a warm light which bade her welcome. She put the boy on the bed, and covered the coals with ashes, for it was hot and close in the house. Then she lighted the piece of candle, and setting it where it could serve her with its light, and yet not shine into his eyes, she proceeded with her work.

Women who live such lives as hers must learn a little of all things, and she knew the duties of a surgeon. Twice she had bound up the wounds of her husband, received in some mountain fray. She undressed the young soldier, and as she did she noticed the scar of a year-old wound under the shoulder,—a wound that might well have been mortal. The bullet of tonight had gone almost through, and she could feel it against the skin on the other side. She cut it out easily with the blade of a pocketknife, and put it in the cupboard. Then she bound up the wound the late bullet had made when it entered, leaving the congealed blood upon it as help against a fresh flow, and sat down to wait.

He was still talking, saying words that had no meaning, and threw his arms about a little; but he was stronger, and she hoped, though she knew, too, that he trembled on the edge.

She sat for a long time watching every movement, even the slightest. The little clock ticked so loudly that she thought once of stopping it; but the sound was so steady and regular that it lulled them, the boy as well as herself, and she let it alone.

He became quieter and grew stronger, too, as she could tell by his breathing, and slept. She spread a sheet over him, and opened the window that a little air might enter the close, warm room. She stood there for a while and looked toward the battlefield, but she could see nothing now to tell her of the combat. The vapors that floated over it hid it and all its ruin.

The wind rose, stirring the hot, close air and cooling the night. It whistled softly through the trees and among the hills, but it did not bring the smell of battle. That had vanished with the combat that had been so unreal itself, as she looked at it from her window. Now she could not see a human figure nor any sign of war. The cabin was just the same lone cabin among the hills that it had always been. She went outside and made the circuit of the house, but there was nothing for eye or ear to note. The night was darkening again, the wind had blown up clouds which hid the face of the moon, and but a few stars twinkled in the sky. The air felt damp, and scattered drops of rain whirled before the wind which was whistling, far off, as it drove away through the hills.

She went back into the house,—for she could not leave the boy more than a minute or two,—and found that he was sleeping well. She prepared some stimulants, and put them where they would be ready to her hand. Then she made over all her arrangements for the morrow, for two instead of one, and placed everything about the house in order, that it might put on its best look in the daylight. She finished her task, and sat down by the bed. Presently the sufferer began to talk of battle and strive to move, thinking he was in action on the field again. When she felt of his wrist and forehead, she saw that the fever was rising, and she thought he was going to die. She did all that her experience told her, and waited. Her bitterness came back, and she called them fools and barbarians once more; she was a fool herself to have had pity upon them.

The boy's wild talk was all of war. She followed through march and camp, skirmish and battle, charge and retreat, and saw how they had taken their hold upon him, and what courage and energy he had put into his part. In half an hour he became quieter, and the fever sank. A cannon-shot boomed among the hills—so far away that the sound was softened by the distance. But it echoed long; hill and valley took it up and passed it on to farther hill and valley; and she heard it again and again, until it died away in the farthest hills like the last throb of a distant drumbeat. It was as if it had been a minute gun for the dead, and she went in terror to the bed; but the boy was not dead. He had passed again from delirium to sleep, and, fearing everything now, she went outside to see if the cannon-shot, by any chance, foretold a renewal of the battle; but it must have been a stray shot, for, as before, nowhere could she see a light, nowhere a living figure, nor could she hear any sound of human beings. The air was cooler, and, shivering, she went back into the house.

Presently, the drops changed to steady rain, which beat upon the windows; but it was peaceful and sheltered in the little house, and as she looked out at the rain, dashed past by the wind, there was a softness in her heart. The rain ceased after a while, and the trees and bushes dripped silver drops. The boy stirred; but it was some thought in his sleep that made him stir, not fever. She looked at him closely. His breathing was regular and easy, and she knew that he would live.

Going once more to the window, and with eyes to the skies, she gave her wordless thanks to God.

A broad bar of light appeared in the east. The day was coming.

Chapter 2

After the Battle

The falling dusk quenched the fury of the battle. The cannon glimmered but feebly on the dim horizon like the sputter of a dying fire. The shouts of combatants were unheard, and Dave Joyce concluded that the fighting was over for that day at least. In his soul he was glad of it.

"Pardner," he said to the wounded man, "the battle has passed on an' left us here like a canoe stuck on a sand bank. I think the fightin' is over, but if it ain't we're out of it anyhow, an' I don't know any law why we shouldn't make ourselves as comf'table as things will allow."

"If there's anythin' done," said the wounded man, "you'll have to do it, for I can't walk, an' I can't move, except when there's a bush for me to grab hold of and pull myself along by."

"That's mighty bad," said Joyce, sympathetically. "Where did you say that bullet took you?"

"I got it in my right leg here," the other replied, "an' I think it broke the bone. Leastways the leg ain't any more use to me than if it was dead, though it hurts like tarnation sometimes. I guess it'll be weeks before I walk again."

"Maybe I could do somethin' for you," said Joyce, "if there was a little more light. I guess I'll take a look, anyhow. I haven't been two years in the army not to know anythin' about bullet wounds."

He bent down and with his pocket-knife cut away a patch of the faded blue cloth from the wounded man's leg.

"I guess I'd better not fool with that," he said, looking critically at the wound. "The bullet's gone all the way through, but the blood's clotted up so thick over the places that the bleedin' has stopped. You won't die if you don't move too much an' start that wound to bleedin' again."

"That's consolin'," said the wounded man; "but, since I can't move, I don't know what's to become of me but to lay here on the field an' die anyway."

"Don't you fret," said Joyce cheerfully. "I'll take care of you. You're Fed. And I'm Confed., but you're hurt an' I ain't, an' if the case was the other way I'd expect you to do as much for me. Besides, I've lost my regiment in the shuffle, and the chances are if I tried to find it again to-night I'd run right into the middle of the Yankee army, and that would mean Camp Chase for your humble servant, which is a bunk he ain't covetin' very bad just now. So I guess it'll be the safe as well as the right thing for me to do to stick by you. Jerusalem! Listen to that! Just hear them crickets chirpin', will you!"

There was a blaze of light in the west, followed by a crash which seemed to roll around the horizon and set all the trees of the forest to trembling. When the echoes were lost beyond the hills the silence became heavy and portentous. The night was hot and sticky, and the powdery vapor that still hung over the field crept into Joyce's throat and made him cough for breath.

"Thunderation!" he said at length, still looking in the direction in which the light had blazed up. "I guess at least a dozen of the big cannon must have been fired at once then. Can't some fellows get enough fightin' in the daytime, without pluggin' away in the night-time too? Now I come of fightin' stock myself—I'm from Kentucky—but twelve hours out of the twenty-four always 'peared to me to be enough for that sort of thing. Besides, it's so infernal hot to-night, too."

"It was hotter than this for me a while ago," said the wounded man.

"So it was, so it was," said Joyce, apologetically, "an' I mustn't forget you, either. Let 'em fight over there if they want to, an' if they're big enough fools to spile a night that way when they might be restin'. What you need just now is water. I think there's a spring runnin' out of the side of that hill there. If you'll listen you'll hear it tricklin' away, so cool and refreshin' like. I guess it was tricklin' that same way, just as calm an' peaceful as Sunday mornin', while the battle was goin' on round here. Don't you feel as if a little water would help you mightily, pardner?"

"'Twould so," said the wounded man. "I'm burnin' up inside, an' if you'd get me a big drink of it I'd think you were mighty nigh good enough to be one of the twelve apostles."

"It's easy enough for me to do it," said Joyce. "I'll be back in a minute."

He took off his big slouch hat and walked toward the source of the trickling sound. From beneath an overhanging rock in the side of the hill near by a tiny stream of water flowed. After a fall of five feet it plunged into a little basin which it had hollowed out for itself in the rock, and formed a deep and cool little pool. Around the edge of the pool the tender green grass grew. The overflow from it wandered away in a little rill through the woods.

"Thunder, but ain't this purty?" exclaimed Joyce, forgetting that the wounded man was out of hearing. "It's just like our springhouse back in old Kentuck. I've put our butter-crocks an' milk-buckets a hundred times to cool in our pool when I was a boy. Wish I had some of them things now!"

The stirring of peaceful memories caused Joyce to linger a little, in forgetfulness of the wounded man. It was cool in the shadow of the hill, and the gay little stream tinkled merrily in his ears. He would have liked to remain there, but he pulled himself together with an impatient jerk, filled the crown of his hat with the limpid water, and started back to the relief of the wounded man.

He followed the channel of the stream for a little way, and as he turned to step across it he noticed the increasing depth of its waters.

"It's dammed up," he muttered. "I wonder what's done that."

"Then he started back shuddering and spilled half the water from his hat, for he had almost stepped on the body of a man that had fallen across the channel of the poor little rivulet, checking the flow of its waters and deepening the stream.

The body lay face downward, and Joyce could not see the wound that had caused death. But as he stooped down he saw again the broad red flash in the west, and heard the heavy crash of the cannon.

"Will them cannon always be hungry?" he muttered. "But I guess I must give this poor little stream which ain't done no harm to anybody the right of way again."

He stooped and pulled the body to one side. With a thankful rush and gurgle the waters of the recent pool sped on in their natural channel, and Joyce returned to the fountain-head to fill his hat again.

He found the wounded man waiting with patience.

"I was gone longer than I ought to have been. Did you think I had left you, pardner?" asked Joyce.

"No," said the man. "I didn't believe you'd play that kind of a trick on me."

"An' so I haven't," said Joyce, "an' for your faith in me, I've brought you a hatful of the nicest an' freshest an' coolest water you ever put your lips to in all your born days. Raise your head up, there, an' drink."

The wounded man drank and drank, and then when the hat was emptied he laid his head back in the grass and sighed as if he were in heaven.

"I must say that you 'pear to like water, pardner," said Joyce.

"Like it?" said the wounded man. "Wait till you've been wounded, an' then you'll know what is to want water. Why, till you brought it I felt as if my inside was full of hot coals and I'd burn all up if I didn't get something mighty quick to put the fire out".

"Then I reckon I've stopped a whole conflagration," said Joyce, "an' with mighty little trouble to myself, too. But I don't wonder that you get thirsty on a night like this. Thunderation, but ain't it clammy!"

He sat down on a fallen tree and drew his coat-sleeve across his brow. Then he held up the sleeve: it was wet with sweat. There was no wind. The night had brought no coolness. The thick and heavy atmosphere hung close to the earth and coiled around and embraced everything. Through it came the faint gun powdery vapor that crept into the throats and nostrils of the two men.

"I wish I was at home sleepin' on the hall floor," said Joyce. "I'll bet it would be cool there."

The wounded man made no answer, but turned his face up to the sky and drew in great mouthfuls of the warm air.

"Them tarnation fools over yonder 'pear to have their dander up yet," said Joyce, pointing to the west, where the alternate flashing and rumbling showed that the battle still lingered. "I thought the battle was over long ago, but I guess it ain't. I've knowed some all-fire fools in my time, but the fellows that would keep on fightin' on a hot night like this must be the all-firedest."

Then the two lay quite still for a while, watching the uneasy rising and falling of the night battle. Had they not known so much of war, they might have persuaded themselves that the flashes they saw were flashes of heat-lightning and the rumbling but the rumbling of summer thunder. But they knew better. They knew it was men and not the elements that fought.

"It's mighty curious," said Joyce, "how the sand's all gone out of me for the time. To-day I felt as if I could whip the whole Yankee army all by myself. To-night I don't want to fight anythin'. I'm as peaceful in temper as a little lamb friskin' about in our old field at home. I hope that there fightin' won't come our way; at least not to-night. How are you feelin', pardner?"

"Pretty well for a wounded man," replied the other; "but I'd like to have some more water."

"Then I'm the man to get it for you," said Joyce, springing up. "An' I'm goin' to see if I can't get somethin' to eat, too, for my innards are cryin' cupboard mighty loud. There's dead men layin' aroun' here, an' there may be somethin' in their haversacks. I hate to rob the dead, but if they've got grub we need it more'n they do."

He returned with another hatful of water, which the wounded man drank eagerly, gratefully. Then he went back and searched in the grass and bushes for the fallen. Presently he came in great glee, and triumphantly held up two haversacks.

"Luck, pardner!" he exclaimed. "Great luck! Bully luck! One of these I got off a dead Fed. and t'other off a dead Confed., and both must have been boss foragers, for in one haversack there's a roast chicken an' in t'other there's half a b'iled ham, an' in both there's plenty of bread. I haven't had such luck before in six months. You're a Yank, pardner, and a Northerner, an' maybe you don't know much about the vanities of roast chicken an' cold b'iled ham. But it's time you did know. I've come from the field at home when I'd been plowin' all day, an' my appetite was as sharp as a razor an' as big as our barn. I'd put up old Pete, our black mule that I'd been plowin' with, an' feed him; then I'd go to the house and kinder loosen my waist-ban', an' mother would say to me, 'Come in the kitchen, Dave; your supper's ready for you.' Say, pardner, you ought to see me then. There'd be a pitcher of cold buttermilk from the spring-house, and one dish of roast chicken, an' another of cold ham, an' all for me too. An' say, pardner, I can taste that ham now. When you eat one piece you want another, an' then another, an' you keep on till there ain't any left on the dish, an' then you lean back in your chair an' wish that when you come to die you'd feel as happy as you do then. Pardner, I wish them times was back again."

"I wish so too," said the wounded man.

"We can't have 'em back, at least not now," said Joyce, cheerily, "but we an make believe, an' it'll be mighty good make-believe, too, for we've got the ham an' the chicken, an' we can get cold water to take the place of cold milk. I guess you can use your arms all right; so you can spread this ham an' chicken out on the grass, an' I'll see if I can't find a canteen to keep the water in. Say, pardner, we'll have a banquet, you an' me, that's what we'll have."

The stalwart young fellow, full of boyish delight at the idea that the thought of home had suggested to him, swung off in search of the canteen. He found not one alone, but two. Then he returned clanking them together to indicate his success. As he came up he called out, in his hearty voice:

"Pardner, is the supper-table ready?" Have you got the knives an' forks? You needn't min' about the napkins. I guess we can get along without 'em just this once."

"All ready," said the wounded man; "an' I guess I can keep you company at this ham an' chicken an' bread, for I'm gettin' a mighty sharp edge on my appetite too."

"So much the better," said Joyce. "There's plenty for both, an' it wouldn't be good manners for me to eat by myself."

He sat down on the grass in front of the improvised repast, and placed one canteen beside the wounded man and the other beside himself.

"Now, pardner," he said, "we'll drink to each other's health, an' then we'll charge the ham an' chicken with more vim than either of us ever charged a breastwork."

They drank from the canteens; and then they made onslaught upon the provisions. Joyce ate for a while in deep and silent content, forgetting the heat and the battle which still lowered in the west. But presently, when his appetite was dulled, he remembered the cannonade.

"There they go again!" he said. "Boom! Boom! Boom! Won't them fellows ever get enough? I thought I was hungry, but the cannon over there 'pear to be hungrier. I suppose there ain't men enough in all this country to stop up their iron throats. But bang away! They don't bother us, do they, pardner? They can't spile this supper, for all their boomin' an' flashin'."

The wounded man bowed assent and took another piece of the ham.

Joyce leaned back on the grass, held up a chicken leg in his hand, and looked contemplatively at it.

"Ain't it funny, pardner," he said, "that you, a Tommy Yank, an' me, a Johnny Reb, are sittin' here, eatin' grub together, as friendly as two brothers, when we ought to be killin' each other? I don't know what Jeff Davis an' old Abe Lincoln will say about it when they hear of the way you an' me are doin'."

The wounded man laughed.

"You can say that I was your prisoner," he said, "when they summon you before the court-martial. An' so I am, if you choose to make me. I can't resist."

"I'm thinkin' more about gettin' back safe to our army than makin' prisoners," said Joyce, as he flung the chicken bone, now bare, into the bushes.

"That may be hard to do," said the wounded man; "for neither you nor me can tell which way the armies will go. Listen to that boomin'! Wasn't it louder than before? That fightin' must be movin' round nearer to us."

"Let it move," said Joyce. "I tell you I've had enough of fightin' for one day. That battle can take care of itself. I won't let it bother me. I don't want to shoot anybody."

"Is that the way you feel when you get into battle?" asked the wounded man.

"I can't say exactly," replied Joyce. "Of course when I go out in a charge with my regiment I want to beat the other fellows, but I don't hate 'em, no, not a bit. I've got nothin' against the Yanks. I've knowed some of 'em that was mighty good fellows. There ain't any of 'em that I want to kill. No, I'll take that back; there is one, just one, a bloody villain that I'd like to draw a bead on an' send a bullet through his skulkin' body."

"Who is that?" asked the wounded man; "an' why do you make an exception of him?"

Joyce remained silent for a moment or two and drew a long blade of grass restlessly through his fingers.

"It's not a pleasant story," he said at last, "an' it hurts me now to tell it, but I made you ask the question, an' I guess I might as well tell you, 'cause I feel friendly toward you, pardner, bein' as we are together in distress, like two Robinson Crusoes, so to speak."

The wounded man settled himself in the grass like one who is going to listen comfortably to a story.

"It's just a yarn of the Kentuck hills," said Joyce, "an' a bad enough one, too. We're a good sort of people up there, but we're hot blooded, an' when we get into trouble, as we sometimes do, kinfolks stan' together. I guess you're from Maine, or York State, or somewhere away up North, an' you can't understand us. But it's just as I say. Sometimes two men up in our hills fight, an' one kills the other. Then the dead man's brothers, an' sons if he's got any old enough, an' cousins, an' so on, take up their guns an; go huntin' for the man that killed him. An' the livin' man's brothers an' sons an' cousins an' so on take up their guns an come out to help him. An' there you've got your feud, an' there's no tellin how many years it'll run on, an' how many people will get killed in it.—Thunderation, but wasn't them cannon loud that time! The battle is movin' round toward us sure!"

Joyce listened a moment, but heard nothing more except the echoes.

"Our family got into one of them feuds," he said. "It was the Joyces and the Ryders. I'm Dave Joyce, the son of Henry Joyce. I don't remember how the feud started; about nothin' much. I guess; but it was a red-hot one, I can tell you, pardner. It was fought fair for a long time, but at last Bill Ryder shot father from ambush and killed him. Father hadn't had much to do with the feud, either; he didn't like that sort of thing—didn't think it was right. I said right then if I ever found the chance when I got big enough I'd kill Bill Ryder."

"Did you get the chance?" asked the wounded man.

"No," replied Joyce. "Country got too hot for Ryder, and he went away. He came back after a while, an I was big enough to go gunnin' for him then, but the war broke out, an' off he went into the Union army before I could get a chance to draw a bead on him. I ain't heard of him since. Maybe he's been killed in battle an' his bones are bleachin' somewhere in the woods."

"Most likely," said the wounded man.

"There's no tellin'," said Joyce. "Still, some day when we're comin' up against the Yanks face to face I may see him before me, an' then I'll hold my gun steady an' shoot straight at him, instead of whoopin' like mad an' firin' lickety-split into the crowd, aimin' at nothin,' as I generally do."

"It's a sad story, very sad for you," said the wounded man.

"Yes," said Joyce. "You don't have such things as feuds up North, do you?"

"No," replied the other, "an' we're well off without 'em. Hark, there's the cannon again!"

"Yes, an' they keep creepin' round toward us with their infernal racket," said Joyce. "Cannon love to chaw up people an' then brag about it. But if them fellows are bent on fightin' all night I guess we'll have to give 'em room for it. What do you say to movin? I've eat all I want, an' I guess you have too, an' we can take what's left with us."

"I don't know," said the wounded man. "My leg's painin' me a good deal an' the grass is soft an' long here where I'm layin'. It makes a good bed, an' maybe I'd better stay where I am."

"I think not," said Joyce decidedly. "That night fight's still swingin' down on us, an' if we stay too long them cannon'll feed on us too. We'd better move, pardner. Let me take a look at your wound. It's gettin' lighter, an' I can see better now. The moon's up, an' she's shinin' for all she's worth through them trees. Besides, them cannon-flashes help. Raise up your head, pardner, an' we'll take a look at your wound together."

"I don't think you can do any good," said the wounded man. "It would be better not to disturb it."

"But we must be movin' pardner," said Joyce, a little impatiently. "See, the fight's warmin' up, an' it's still creepin' down on us. Seems to me I can almost hear the tramp of the men an' the rollin' of the cannon-wheels. Jerusalem! What a blaze that was! I say, it's time for us to be goin'. If we stay here we're likely to be ground to death under the cannon-wheels, if we ain't shot first. Just let me get a grip under your shoulders, pardner, an' I'll take you out of this."

The cannon flamed up again, and the deep thunder filled all the night.

"Listen how them old iron throats are growlin' an' mutterin'," said Joyce; "an' they're sayin' it's time for us to be travelin'."

"I believe," said the wounded man, "that I would rather stay where I am an' take my chances. If I move I'm afraid I'll break open my wound. Besides, I think you're mistaken. It seems to me that the fight's passin' round to the right of us."

"Passin' to the right of us nothin'," said Joyce. "It's coming straight this way, with no more respect for our feelin's than if you an' me was a couple of field-mice."

The wounded man made no answer.

"Do you think, pardner," asked Joyce, slight offence showing in his voice, "that the Yanks may come this way an' pick you up an' then you won't be a prisoner? Is that your game?"

As his companion made no answer, Joyce continued:

"You don't think, pardner, that I want to hold you a prisoner, do you? An' you a wounded man, too, that I picked up on the battle-field and that I've eat and drank with? Why, that ain't my style."

He waited for an answer, and as none came he was seized with a sudden alarm.

"You ain't dead, pardner?" he cried. "Jerusalem! What if he's died while I've been standin' here talkin' an' wastin' time!"

He bent over to take a look at the other's face, but the wounded man, with a sudden and convulsive movement, writhed away from him and struck at him with his open hand.

"Keep away!" he cried. "Don't touch me! Don't come near me! I won't have it! I won't have it!"

"Thunderation, pardner!" exclaimed Joyce; "what do you mean? I ain't goin' to harm you. I want to help you." Then he added, pityingly, "I guess he's got the fever an' gone out of his head. So I'll take him along whether he wants to go or not."

He bent over again, seized the wounded man by the shoulders, and forcibly raised him up. At the same moment the cannonade burst out afresh and with increased violence. A blaze of light played over the face of the wounded man, revealing and magnifying every feature, every line.

Joyce uttered no exclamation, but he dropped the man as if he had been a coiling serpent in his hands, and looked at him, an expression of hate and loathing creeping over his face.

"So, he said, at last, "this is the way I have found you?"

The wounded man lay as he had fallen, with his face to the earth.

"No wonder," said Joyce, "you wanted to keep your face hid in the grass! No wonder you hide it there now!"

"Oh, Dave! Dave!" exclaimed the man, springing to his knees with sudden energy, "don't kill me! Don't kill me, Dave!"

"Why shouldn't I kill you?" asked Joyce, scornfully. "What reason can you give why I shouldn't do it?"

"There ain't any. There ain't any. Oh, I know there ain't any," cried the wounded man. "But don't do it, Dave! For Christ's sake don't do it!"

"You murderer! You sneakin', ambushin' murderer! said Joyce. "It's right for you to beg for your life an' then not get it! Hear them cannon! Hear how they growl, an' see the flash from their throats! They'd like to feed on you, but they won't. That sort of death is too good for the likes of you. The death for you is to be shot like a ravin' cur."

He drew the loaded pistol from his belt and cocked it with deliberate motion.

"Dave! Dave!" the man cried, dragging himself to Joyce's feet, "you won't do that! You can't! It would be murder, Dave, to shoot me here, me a wounded man that can't help myself!"

"You done it, an' worse," said Joyce. "Of all the men unburnt in hell I think the one who deserves to be there most is the man who hid in ambush and shot another in the back that had never harmed him."

"I know it, Dave, I know it!" cried the wounded man, grasping Joyce's feet with both hands. "It was an awful thing to do, an' I've been sorry a thousand times that I done it, but all the sorrow in the world an' everythin' else that's in the world can't undo it now."

"That's so," said Joyce, "but it don't make any reason why the murderer ought to be kept on livin'."

"It don't, Dave; you're right, I know; but I don't want to die!" cried the man. "I'm a coward, Dave, and I don't want to die by myself here in the woods an' in the dark!"

"You'll soon have light enough," said Joyce, "an' I won't shoot you."

He let down the hammer of his pistol and replaced the weapon on his belt.

"Oh, Dave! Dave! exclaimed the man, kissing Joyce's foot, "I'm so glad you'll let me have my life. I know I ain't fit to live, but I want to live anyhow."

"I said I wouldn't shoot you," said Joyce, "but I never said I'd spare your life. See that blaze in the trees up there."

A few hundred yards away the forest had burst into flame. Sparks fell upon a tree and blazed up. Long red spirals coiled themselves around the trunk and boughs until the tree became a mass of fire, and then other tongues of flame leaped forward and seized other trees. There was a steady crackling and roaring, and the wind that had sprung up drove smoke and ashes and fiery particles before it.

"That," said Joyce, "is the wood on fire. Them cannon that's been makin' so much fuss done it. I've seen it often in battle when the cannon have been growlin'. The fire grows an' it grows, an' it burns up everythin' in its way. The army is still busy fightin', an' the wounded, them that's hurt too bad to help themselves, have to lay there on the ground an' watch the fire comin', an' sure to get 'em. By an' by it sweeps down on 'em, an' they shriek an' shriek, but that don't do no good, for before long the fire goes on, an' there they are, dead an' burnt to a coal. I tell you it's an awful death!"

The wounded man was silent now. He had drawn himself up a little, and was watching the fire as it leaped from tree to tree and devoured them one after another.

"That fire is comin' for us, an' the wind is bringin' it along fast," said Joyce, composedly, "but it's easy enough for me to get out of its way. All I've got to do is to go up the hill, an' the clearin's run for a long way beyond. I can stay up there an' watch the fire pass, an' you'll be down here right in its track."

"Dave!" cried the man, "you ain't goin to let me burn to death right before your eyes?"

"That's what I mean to do," said Joyce. "I don't like to shoot a wounded man that can't help himself, an' I won't do it, but I ain't got no call to save you from another death."

"I'd rather be shot than burned to death," cried the man in a frenzy.

"It's just the death for you," said Joyce.

Then the wounded man again dragged himself to the feet of Joyce.

"Don't do it, Dave!" he cried. "Don't leave me here to burn to death! Oh, I tell you, Dave, I ain't fit to die!"

"Take your hands off my feet," said Joyce. "I don't want 'em to touch me. There's too much blood on 'em."

"Don't leave me to the fire!" continued the man. "You've been kind to me to-night. Help me a little more, Dave, an' you'll be glad you done it when you come to die yourself!"

"I must be goin'," said Joyce, repulsing the man's detaining hands. "It's gettin' hot here now, an' that fire will soon be near enough to scorch my face. Good-by."

"For the sake of your own soul, Dave Joyce," cried the man, beating the ground with his hands, "don't leave me to burned to a coal! Think, Dave, how we eat and drank together to-night, like two brothers, an' how you waited on me an' brought the water an' the grub. You'll re-member them things, Dave, when you come to die yourself!"

The fire increased in strength and violence. The flames ran up the trees, and whirled far above them in red coils that met and twined with each other, and then whirled triumphantly on in search of fresh fuel. A giant oak, burned through at the base and swept of all its young boughs and foliage, fell with a rending crash, a charred and shattered trunk. The flames roared, and the burning trees maintained an incessant crackling like a fire of musketry. The smoke through which the sparks of fire were sown in millions grew stifling.

"God, what a sight!" cried Joyce.

"Dave, you won't leave me to that?" cried Ryder.

Joyce drew down his hat over his eyes to shield them from the smoke. Then he stooped, lifted the wounded man upon his powerful shoulders, and went on over the hill.

Chapter 3

The Break of Day

"And you feel sure that the attack will be made before morning?" asked Carson.

"Undoubtedly," replied Beltone. "They know that our defenses are imperfect and that we have lost heavily. They will not give us time to strengthen ourselves."

"Can we beat them off?"

"I do not think we can stop them. I would not say this before the men, but I will to you. They appear to be in force much superior to ours. Besides, they are just as good, man for man, as we are. They have shown that here as well as many a time elsewhere. Did you notice the tall, slender man, with the scar across his face, who was in the front of the charge they made this morning?"

"The one who climbed upon the breastwork at the left angle?"

"Yes. Right in the mouth of our guns. Even after the attack was repulsed he leaned over and chopped at our cannoneers with his sword until some of the men seized him and dragged him inside, a prisoner. When they have the advantage of numbers and of darkness to render our aim ineffective we cannot overcome such desperate courage as that."

"But we may be reinforced."

"Improbable. We have been tangled up a long time in the wilderness. The movement was well intended, but it has failed; and now we are like a mislaid and forgotten package in this lonely isolated spot. Remember how long it has been since we have heard from the army. We do not even know which way it has gone."

"You don't take a cheerful view of the matter."

"I was merely presenting the facts. But don't look upon me as a croaking raven, predicting evil, old fellow. There are no cowards in our party, and I dare say we shall give a good account of ourselves. Only, as the last hand in the game is to be played soon, I wish our hand was as good as theirs."

The two young officers shrank close to the rude and hastily thrown up earthwork as they whispered together. The darkness, heavy, clammy, and thick with the exhalations from the slimy ooze of the swamps, oppressed them. Behind them they could see indistinctly the recumbent forms of some of their comrades catching a little sleep upon the ground. To the right and to the left were the sentinels. In front was the little clearing, and beyond the forest in which the enemy lay. The moon cast down a few pallid rays which apparently served only to make the darkness visible.

"What a black night!"whispered Carson. "This darkness and the swamp ooze creep into my marrow and numb my courage. I have to reinforce my nerves with my will."

"Many a brave man before you has had to do that when old Father Sun has gone down the other side of the earth," returned Beltone. "Fighting is bad enough at any time, but a night attack, barring the noise, is like a battle among the ghosts. Can you see anything over there in the wood?"

"No," said Carson; "I can barely make out the outline of the wood itself. The moon is of very little use tonight. I suppose it is so much ashamed of the war and bloodshed here that it does not consider it worth while to pay any serious attention to this portion of the earth."

"Never mind," said Beltone; "it's the same moon that's shining, or rather not shining, for the enemy over there. So long as the darkness is as thick as this they will not attack. They could not tell friends from enemies."

"They are silent in the wood," resumed Beltone, a moment later. "Such a considerable force lying so very near us makes no noise that we can hear. I should say that circumstance certainly portended an attack. They are resting before the rush. Ah, what is that?"

"You have nerves as well as I," chuckled Carson, "when the hoot of a swamp owl, which you have heard many and many a time before, would disturb you like that."

"I don't deny it," said Beltone, "nor am I ashamed of it. It is hard enough work to lie down with the reserves in a big battle and wait your turn to be called, while you hear the cannon thundering in front, and the wounded are taken by you to the rear, and the Minie balls are zip-zipping over your head. But then you have the bright sun shining over you, and there is no friend like the daylight. Here you crouch in the darkness and wait for a hand to cleave the black veil and strike you."

There was a perfect silence in the camp. In the distant wood, the notes of the night owl rose higher and higher and grew more mournful the higher they rose.

"Isn't that a brooding raven?" whispered Carson. "He makes the lines of that old poem sing through my head."

"It may be the dirge of some brave man," returned Beltone; "again, he may be lamenting man's folly."

"Confound it, I wish he would stop, whatever he means. The swamp and the darkness and the owl together may be too much for me," said Carson.

Beltone did not reply. A faint breeze sprang up, but it brought to them nothing but the rustling of the leaves, and the owl's melancholy measure. The two young men still sat by the earthwork, and tried to pierce the darkness. Presently Beltone said,

"The moon is getting brighter; can you see anything in the wood there now?"

"Nothing except the trees that compose it," returned Carson. "We might send a cannon ball into it. That would stir them up."

"It's not worth while," said Beltone. "They would simply draw further back, if they are not already out of range. There's nothing for us but to wait."

"Beltone," said Carson, "I don't mean to be melodramatic or sentimental, but if I fall you will tell them at home what became of me?"

"Certainly," replied Beltone calmly, even cheerfully, "if you are the one taken and I am the one left. If it is the reverse, I ask you to do as much for me. If we both fall, probably enough of our comrades will be left to make all the history of it the world needs."

They relapsed again into silence, but remained beside the breastwork, voluntary and vigilant sentinels. Old Time moved on with heavy step. The owl's hoot died away, and only the rustling of the wind through the leaves was heard.

"It seems a week since the sun set," said Carson.

"And that means that it will be another week until the sun rises again," returned Beltone. "It must be about midnight now. Do you see anything in the wood yet?"

"No, only the trees swaying in the wind. I think I shall climb upon the breastwork and get a better view."

"Don't do it."

"Why?"

"Sharpshooters. Some of them can see like owls, and the shadows will not protect you."

"I'll chance it."

Cautiously he climbed the earthwork. There was a report from the wood, followed by the familiar singing noise that a Minie ball makes, and Carson rolled back into the camp.

"It is nothing, or rather a narrow escape only, he said getting up. I felt the swish of his bullet past my cheek. I am not hurt."

Beltone made no comment. By and by he asked again.

"Can you see anything yet in the wood?"

"No; nothing but the black wall of trees."

"But don't you hear a sound that is not the rustling of the leaves?"

"I think so, but I can't tell yet whether it's reality or the imagination."

"There, again; don't you hear it?"

"I seem to hear something; but still it may only be imagination playing one of her tricks at the sunset of life."

"If I do not really hear it, then imagination is very strong, even for such a night and such a situation as this."

"The balance is certainly inclining to the side of reality."

"Listen!"

They lay perfectly quiet for a minute, straining every sense to hear. Then Beltone drew his pistol belt a little tighter.

"There can be no doubt of it," he said.

"The wind is blowing from the wood towards us, and in the stillness of the night sound comes a long distance with great distinctness. I have heard such sounds too often before to be mistaken. That steady, regular pulsation could not be made by anything but marching troops."

"It isn't possible that they are withdrawing! Beltone! Do you think they are?"

"No. They have been reinforced. That sound was made by troops coming to join them. It means heavier odds against us when the rush comes. There—do you hear that? Am I not right?"

A cheer, far away and faint, but unmistakable, came to them. In a moment it was repeated, and then again and again, each time swelling with increased volume.

"I don't see why they should make so much noise about it," said Carson, a little pettishly.

"It's their time to cheer," returned Beltone quietly.

After the cheers came silence, and for a long time the listening men could hear nothing. Then a confused hum and murmur of voices came from the wood; but this, too soon died away, and the stillness of the night settled down again. It might have been a half hour afterwards when a plaintive but clear note pierced the air and startled the listening men. As it continued, the sound grew louder and fuller. Mellow and sweet, it filled the darkness around them.

"A violin!" said Carson. "On the eve of battle. How strange!"

"I never knew anything like it before in all my experience of war," returned Beltone. "But hush, listen. Don't you recognize the tune?"

Through the heavy night air floated the solemn strains of "Home, Sweet Home," and the music rose and fell as if the hand of a master held the bow.

"Perhaps the forest is haunted," whispered Carson.

"If it's not, the force out there has a strange commander!" returned Beltone. "He has an odd method of rousing the spirits of the men for battle."

"Beltone," said Carson gravely, "don't forget your promise about telling them at home, if I fall in the morning."

Before Beltone could reply a voice, deep in the wood, took up the strain of the violin and blended with its notes. Over them and around them, clear and sweet, floated the words and the echo of the song:

> Home, home, sweet home,
> Be it ever so humble,
> There's no place like home.

The atmosphere had cleared and the moon shone bright. Beltone could see a tear glisten on the eyelid of his companion.

"Do not be ashamed of it," said Beltone, with a nervous little laugh, as Carson raised his hand to wipe the tear away. "When we lose our feelings we cease to be men."

He stopped for now a dozen, twenty, even fifty—yes, a hundred voices, far away in the wood, joined in the song of home.

Then the melody ceased. Beltone heard a sigh of regret, like an echo, from Carson.

Neither spoke for some time. Then Carson said.

"Beltone, what does it mean?"

"I cannot say. Perhaps it was for amusement. But I would choose another kind of music for troops who expected to make a bloody assault in an hour or two. Still, you never can tell what a commander will do. The sternest of them grow sentimental sometimes."

Beltone shrugged his shoulders, and the two again relapsed into their silent waiting. But they heard the music no more.

"What we shall hear next will be music of a different sort," said Carson.

The night crept on with heavier steps than ever.

"Daylight cannot be far away. The enemy's rush is near at hand. We are as well prepared for him as we can be in this camp here. But I wish it were all over."

"I believe I hear their footsteps now," said Carson. "Listen. Are they coming?"

But the sound, if there was any, died away, and the two men crouched against the soft earth, waited, and heard nothing.

A slight gray streak appeared in the east. It broadened, and soon bars of light shot up over the forest.

"He will come now," whispered Beltone, "when there is just light enough for him to see our camp, and too little for us to take aim by."

But the wood was still silent. No human forms could be seen among the trees. The bars of light broadened. The red edge of the sun arose above the horizon. A full throated bird in a tree began to sing.

"Strange," said Beltone. "Where is he? He is not wont to be lax like this."

The morning grew, until camp and forest and swamp were flooded with the yellow sunlight.

Suddenly Carson grasped Beltone's arm.

"There is some one," he said. "They are coming at last!"

A man appeared at the edge of the clearing. He held up his hands and walked towards the camp. He was unarmed.

Beltone and Carson watched him intently. The rifles of the sentinels covered him.

"I wonder what he is after? Does he want to play with us after the cat-and-mouse fashion?" muttered Beltone.

The man came on towards the camp. Other men fell in behind him, but came no further than the edge of the wood. The stranger walked with an easy step, straight and firm, toward the earthwork where Beltone and Carson stood, awaiting his approach.

"An officer of rank. A colonel, at least," said Beltone.

The stranger saluted.

"I wish you a pleasant morning sirs,"

"We are indebted to you. I trust you are well," said Beltone, with equal politeness. "May I ask you who has honored us with this visit?"

"Certainly." He spoke with great dignity. "I am Colonel Walton of the Louisiana troops, commander of the forces out there."

"I have heard of you often, colonel," returned Beltone. "We have not forgotten how you held us back that fierce day at the bend of the river."

"I have done the best that I could for what I thought was right," said the colonel simply.

Then Beltone asked,

"Have you any message that I may take to our commander?"

"Yes," said Colonel Walton. "We were joined by Tennessee troops last night. Their officers are fine fellows, and they bring us news. Perhaps you heard us singing in the night?"

"Yes," said Beltone wonderingly.

"Well then," the stranger continued, "say to your commander that I and my officers would be greatly pleased and honored if he and his staff would take dinner with us today. It is true that we have little to offer, but I dare say we can treat you well."

"Why, sir," said Beltone angrily, "what sort of jesting is this? We are aware that you are in overwhelming force, but before we go into your camp as prisoners you must first come and take us. War is bad enough, sir, without such ill timed jokes as this."

"War?" said Colonel Walton calmly. Why do you speak of war? General Lee and his army surrendered three days ago, The war is over.

Chapter 4

Guard No. 10

Guard No. 10 walked back and forth before the open gate, waiting until the wagon should go out again. It was a dim, gray day of February, the air full of damp chill and a raw wind blowing. The clouds that turned the skies to the color of rusty steel told of snow or sleet somewhere. Beyond the walls the dead weeds rustled sadly as the cold wind blew upon them, and over the yellow ponds tiny waves pursued each other. Across the wastes the wind moaned.

Inside the heavy stone walls of the military prison was some life, but not the life of good cheer. Coils of languid blue smoke arose from the squalid huts in which the prisoners lived. A dozen of them strolled along the rough road that ran between the huts like the street of some shambling village. Some wore the dingy gray uniforms in which they had been taken, ragged and patched, and others were wrapped in blankets from their beds. All were thin and pale.

Guard No. 10 did not look long at the prisoners; it was too old a sight to stir any emotion in him, a man who was not given to abstruse thought, and who had feelings only of the primitive order. His own figure was in accord with the prison, with its granite walls, dark and stained by time, with the rude huts, the bleak yard, and the wasted, hopeless men. He was short, thick set, wrapped in an old blue overcoat, his face stained like the stone walls about him by all kinds of weather.

He walked back and forth, back and forth, without ceasing, always turning at the same place, and always making his steps of equal length. His blue overcoat and blue cap were the color of the steel blue sky above him. He carried his rifle across his shoulder and held the stock with a firm hand. His figure added the most somber touch to the somber scene.

Guard No. 10 continued to walk monotonously back and forth, and drew up the collar of his overcoat, for the wind was rising and the air grew colder. Most of the prisoners returned to their huts, and the guard would have gone on his mechanical way had not a prisoner spoken to him in a weak voice. He ordered him back roughly, telling him he was not allowed to approach the gate: but the man said he only wished to see the outside of a prison, a sight that had been denied to him for a year.

"Just to remind me of what I used to be," he said with a weak little laugh.

Guard No. 10 looked at him more closely. He had noticed this prisoner before, one of the most pathetic figures in a place that was full of them. He was not a man, only a boy of seventeen or eighteen, young enough to be Guard No. 10's son, slim and fair like a girl, weak from prison air, bad food, and old wounds just healed.

"I saw that the gate was open," he said appealingly, "and I wanted to take a look at the country outside, just to see the grass and the woods again: it's been a long time since I saw them."

"The grass is dead," said the guard roughly. "It's had a winter to kill it, and there isn't a leaf on the trees."

"Do you think I care for that?" said the boy. "It's because there are no prison walls around them."

He stood where he was, twenty feet from the gate and the guard did not order him away.

"I could break him in two across my knee if I tried," thought Guard No. 10.

The air from the free world outside blew through the open gate and the boy breathed it gratefully. Guard No. 10 kept his eye on him and held his rifle ready. If any prisoner dared to make a dash for freedom he knew his duty and would do it. The boy spoke to him again and then again, but the guard was stern and did not reply. The boy looked at the man with an appeal in his face. He wished to speak of the world outside, to hear of anything that was not prison talk.

"Well, what do you want?" asked the guard at last, growing tired of the prisoner's reproachful gaze.

"I—I don't know," said the boy, starting at the suddenness of the question. "How is the war going?"

"What is that to you?" asked the guard. "Why were you Southern boys such fools as to go into it?"

"I don't know," replied the boy, in his thin voice. "I don't know what the war is about, do you?"

"No, I don't, except that you Southern fellows are wrong," replied the guard more roughly than ever.

The boy did not seem to resent the reply, as if it were an issue for which he did not care. His pale face had flushed a little under the touch of the free wind that blew in at the open gate, and he opened his mouth as if he would breathe an air purer than that within prison walls. The glimpse, the breath of the free world had a charm for him which the leaden skies, the somber day, and the dreary landscape without could not dispel. Guard No. 10 was impressed more than ever by the weakness of his frame, and the look of homesickness in his eyes.

"They say that down there in the South they have robbed the cradle and the grave to fight this war, and I guess it's true about the cradle," he said.

The boy smiled. He was not hurt at the remark.

"I was fourteen when I went into it," he said, "but there were some younger."

"A mere baby," said Guard No. 10.

"I had been in more than ten battles before I was taken," said the boy proudly.

"But I guess you've had enough," rejoined Guard No. 10.

"Yes, I've had enough," said the boy frankly. "I'm tired of war. I've been here a year, and I'm just getting well from my wounds. I had two of them, one in the shoulder and one in the side." He mentioned his wounds with a little touch of pride. "They are cured, and I'm cured of war, too," he went on, smiling again. "It's the prison life that's done it, and it's the prison life that may end me, too, for though the wounds are healed, I'm mightily run down."

He turned his eyes again toward the open gate, and the look of homesickness in them was stronger than ever. A faint feeling stirred in the breast of Guard No. 10, and he began to think it was wrong for such young boys to go to the war. His curiosity rose a little.

"Where is your home?" he asked.

"In Georgia, in the southern part of the State, near the sea. Oh, it's not gray and cold and bleak like this! It's green all the year round; the sun shines warm and the watermelons grow big and juicy. I've had some high old times there."

"Guess you wish you were there now," said the guard curtly.

The boy's face had flushed with enthusiasm as he spoke, but at the guard's question the flush died out.

"Yes, he said sadly. "I wish I was there. It's too cold for me here; it's not the kind of country I'm used to. The prison doctor says I can't ever get all my strength so long as I stay in this place. But down in the sunshine I'd be all right in a month. I wish I could get exchanged."

"No chance of that," said Guard No. 10. "We're not exchanging much, because we've got more men that you Rebs have and we want to wear you out soon."

Yet pity for the boy was finding small lodgment in the crusty soul of Guard No. 10.

"And the doctor don't think you can get well here?" he asked.

"No," replied the boy. The air of the place and the bad food are against me."

"What are you going to do about it?"

"I think I'll escape," said the boy, with a sad little laugh. "Some dark night when you guards are asleep at your posts, I'll climb over that high stone wall there and skip across the fields."

Guard No. 10 looked at the stone wall rising far above his head, its smooth sides offering no hold for the human foot, and then at the frail figure of the boy.

"I guess you won't climb over that wall in a hurry, even if we guards should go to sleep at our posts, which we never do," he said grimly. "But even if you were to get over the walls, what could you do? You are in the country of your enemies, and it's a long road to Georgia. We'll have you back here inside of twenty four hours."

"Oh, no, you wouldn't," said the boy, in a tone of conviction. "It's only a mile to the town, and I've some friends there, some people who used to live in the South. I could get to their house, for my clothes are not the Confederate gray, and then slip down to Georgia, if these walls were not twenty feet high and two feet thick."

"Yes, that's the trouble," said Guard No. 10. "Now, if they were only fifteen feet high and one foot thick you might make it. But we've got to keep you, for so long as you're not with 'em we've got a chance to beat the Rebs."

He laughed a little. The boy amused him, and added a bit of interest to his lonely watch. But the prisoner's delicate face flushed at the guard's sarcasm.

"Where were you taken?" asked the guard, feeling somewhat sorry for his sneer.

"At Chickamauga."

"And you have been in ten battles? What was your first?"

"Shiloh."

"Shiloh?" said the guard, with a sudden increase of interest. "Why, I was there myself!"

"So you've served at the front too?" said the boy.

"Yes," replied Guard No. 10. "I served until I got a bullet in the thigh at Stone River, that laid me up for three months. I was invalided home, and after a while, sent to this duty. But about Shiloh. That was a hot fight!"

"Hot?" said the boy. "Hot was no name for it! For a while I thought all the men in the world were there shooting at each other; and even now, just as I am about to go to sleep, I often hear the whistling of the bullets."

Guard No. 10 walked back and forth more slowly, and for the first time his seamy brown face showed feeling.

"You're right about the bullets," he said. "All the lead that was shot off then would make a mine. You fellows caught us napping there that Sunday morning. Our generals say it wasn't so, but it was. And Lord, how you came, what a rush! You Johnny Rebs can fight well. I give you that much credit."

"But you got back at us the next day when your reinforcements came up," said the boy. "It was our turn to be driven then."

"Yes, we won back the ground we had lost," said Guard No. 10 meditatively, his mind going back to the details of the great battle. "But I can't forget that first morning when you rushed us. And you were there and I was there, and now we're both here. But it isn't so strange. More than a hundred thousand others were there, too, and some of them are bound to meet some day."

"What did you think when you saw us popping out of the woods and bushes that morning?" asked the boy.

"I didn't have time to think of anything," replied the guard. "It was just a great red and brown veil of fire and smoke, with you fellows showing dimly through it, rushing down upon us, and the noise of the cannon and rifles banging away in our ears, so we couldn't hear each other speak or even shout. It was just grab our guns and fire away, every fellow fighting for himself, or running—mostly running, I guess. But we got together part of our regiment in some fashion or other and tried to make a stand, though you pushed us back and kept pushing us back toward the river. Hot, boy! I should say it was hot, with the rebel bullets whizzing like hail about our ears, and forty thousand rifles and a hundred cannon blazing in our faces! Boy, I don't know where I'm going when I die, but if it comes to the worst it won't be any hotter than it was that morning at Shiloh."

It was the longest speech he had made in a year, but Guard No. 10 felt emotion at memory of the great battle, and as a mark of feeling shifted his gun from his left to his right shoulder. The boy's eyes sparkled for the first time. He, too, was aroused by the memories of Shiloh, and he waited for Guard No. 10 to continue.

"There was one regiment of the rebels that pushed us specially," said the guard; "a Georgia regiment. I saw the name of the State on their banner, and I remember how surprised I was to see that they were mostly blue eyed, light haired men; I used to have an idea before the war that all you Southern fellows were dark. They seemed to have picked us out as their particular meat, and they didn't care whether it was kill or get killed; so it was one or the other. They were brave men, if ever brave men lived. Gunpowder was apple sauce to them. I remember their colonel, funny enough looking for a circus, six feet and a half high, as thin as a rail, his long yellow hair flying back, and his uniform five times too big for him., flapping about him like clothes on a line. But he was the bravest of them all, always in front, waving his long arms and yelling to 'em to come on, though they were coming as fast as they could. He was thunderation ugly, but he was a man all over."

The guard shook his head and laughed, pleased at the recollection. The prisoner laughed, too, and there was heartiness in his tone.

"That bean pole was my colonel," he said, "and that was my regiment. You fellows were eating your breakfast when we rushed out of the woods and burst upon you. We went right through your camp when we drove you back. I remember stopping to drink a cup of hot coffee that one of you left unspilled on the ground. It had been poured out for a Yankee, and a reb drank it before it got cold."

The two laughed together with heartiness and enjoyment.

"And you were there in that regiment of brave men who pushed us so hard?" said Guard No. 10 admiringly.

"Yes," said the boy proudly.

"Then we have fought with each other, you and I, hand to hand?" said the guard.

"Yes, " said the boy.

"And here you are, after such fighting as that, in a military prison."

"Yes," said the boy.

"And the doctor says you will die if you can't get out where you'll have better air and better food?"

"Yes," said the boy sadly.

"And there's no chance of an exchange!"

The boy stood there, a thin figure under the somber sky. The guard looked intently into his eyes, and the prisoner's face grew eager when he met the look.

"That wagon will be here in a minute," said Guard No. 10, "and I mustn't be seen talking to a prisoner."

He shifted his rifle again to his left shoulder and walked to the end of his beat, deliberately turning his back to the open gate. The wind blew dismally, and the guard heard a faint, quick footstep.

The wagon was approaching, and he walked back to the other end of his beat. There was no prisoner in sight. The wagon passed out, and the guard, closing and locking the gate, resumed his march, gun on shoulder.

Chapter 5

The Retreat of the Ten

They stopped at noon beside a shallow brook, more mud than water, to rest, and to eat a little of the cold food in their knapsacks. When the brief meal was ended, Chilton, the Kentuckian, strolled out on the prairie and looked about him.

Except the horses, his was the only upright figure within the circle of the horizon. Far off to the left were patches of squat, thorny bushes, and nearer by ran a fringe of ragged and desolate weeds. Overhead burned a coppery sun, swinging low, and the chief impression upon his mind was that of desolation and loneliness.

"Have I been fighting four years for this?" murmured Chilton.

His eyes followed the circle of the horizon, but everywhere he saw the same—the rolling brown plains, the scanty grass, the desolate weeds and thorn-bush, all shriveling in the fierce rays of the sun. Then he walked back to the brookside.

"How far is it to the border, Chilton?" asked Hicks, the oldest of the party, a thick-set Mississippian of fifty.

"Bloodgood says we ought to make it in three days of hard riding, and he knows the country."

"So we can," said Bloodgood, the Texan, "if the horses don't give out. Texas is a big state and it has good country and bad. This isn't part of the good."

"I should think not," said Chilton, looking again at the sweep of desolation about them. "Let the Yankees have it and welcome, for they'll take it anyhow. Everything's Yankee now from the St. Lawrence to the Rio Grande."

Young Hicks stirred in his sleep and rolled over, where the sun had a fair aim at his face. Old Hicks, his father, put the boy's broad-brimmed hat over his eyes, and, protected from the glare, he slept peacefully on.

The Dupuy brothers, the South Carolinians, rose and began to buckle the girths of their horses. McCormick, the Florida cracker, a long, thin, yellow man, followed them, and the bustle of the start began.

"Wake the boy," said Chilton. "We'd better be going."

"It's time to mount again, Frank," said old Hicks, shaking his son, "and then ho for Mexico!"

"Hurrah for Mexico!" said the boy, with enthusiasm, "and may the deuce take this country, since we couldn't keep the Yankees out of it! We'll never live on this soil or under the Yankee flag again! Let's take an oath on it, pledge our faith to one another. No, let's sign an agreement."

The proposal was boyish like the proposer, but it found favor with the sullen and defiant temper of the men.

"Good enough," said Chilton. "I have a note-book and the stub of an old lead pencil, and I guess they'll do."

So he drew up a rude statement that the undersigned had served four years in the Confederate army, and, being still loyal to their cause, re-fused to live in the Yankee republic. Moreover, they took an oath to do all they could to break it up. Then they swore and signed, the whole ten, the boy first and Chilton last. Chilton folded the paper carefully and put it in an inside pocket of his waistcoat, where he also carried a little purse of American gold.

Then they mounted their horses and rode on. The formal oath of renunciation pleased them and soothed their sullen and angry tempers. These men, one of them fifty years old, began to build air-castles— castles in Mexico.

"If enough of the old Confederates would only go down there," said Taylor, the Georgian, "we might establish, with the start that the country already has, a power which would offset that of the Yankees."

"It's not impossible," said Chilton, meditatively. "We are not the only southerners on the way to Mexico, and as we succeed others will be drawn after us. In a year or two we ought to have at least fifty thousand Confederates about us, and we'll be enough to run things. We'll estab-lish a new power, a great empire, in Mexico."

Their spirits swelled so high that they broke into a gallop, Bloodgood, the Texan, in the lead, as he was to be the guide to the frontier. They rose from the prairie rather late the next morning. The day was gray and not promising. Young Hicks noticed a raw damp in the air that made him shiver. They ate breakfast, and mounting, refreshed themselves with a gallop, and then built more castles in Mexico. But the gray in the air thickened into a mist, and the sun looked pale and sick. Young Hicks shivered and wrapped his army blanket around his shoulders.

The cold increased rapidly and the wind began to blow. It raised clouds of dust and sand which turned into curious shapes, and, whirling after one another across the plain, passed out of sight. The horses snorted with fright and cold. The Ten rode in a close huddle, men and horses rubbing against one another, for the sake both of comradeship and of prudence. They came to a low hill which bore a patch of dwarfed trees and interlacing thorn-bushes, and behind it they found some shelter from the storm, now sweeping the prairie with all the fury of a simoom in the Sahara. The sand and dust were driven before the wind in thick clouds, but most of it passed over their heads now, though it made a whistling and shrieking noise like the sound of flying bullets in battle. The cold was bitter and reached the bone. Rain began to fall, but soon changed to showers of hail which beat upon the men and cut their faces. It was as dark as night.

They remained silent, shivering in their wet clothes, until the norther began to abate. The whistle and shriek of the wind died, the air ceased to be a compound of sand and dust, and the sun, breaking a way at last through the clouds, poured a flood of light over the earth which melted the sheets of hail and turned the temperature in an hour from midwinter to midsummer.

"This is bad on those who have fresh-cured wounds," said Old Hicks to Chilton. He looked anxiously as he spoke at Young Hicks, whose face was pinched and white.

"The boy will stand it all right," said Chilton, confidently. "He's a tough sapling, he is."

Old Hicks seemed to be reassured somewhat, and the Ten rode on. The sunshine was bright enough, and the air warm enough, but Young Hicks was strangely quiet. Presently his teeth began to rattle together.

"He has a chill, a bad one," said Old Hicks to Chilton.

"Then we must stop and doctor him; it's the wet clothes," replied Chilton.

They built a fire of dead bushes, fallen last year, which they coaxed into a blaze, but it did no good; the boy was in the grip of a chill of the very strongest kind, and following the usual course, the icy cold of his body soon began to change to a heat equally fierce.

"We've got to camp," said Chilton to the others. "We can't go on with the boy in this fix."

The lad's fever rose so high that he became delirious, and talked about his home in northern Mississippi which he had not seen in three years.

"Who's there?" asked Chilton of Old Hicks—meaning the place of which the boy talked.

"Nobody but the old lady."

"The old lady?"

"Of course, you don't know—his grandmother, I mean, his mother's mother. His mother died when he was born, and the old lady raised him. She's up there now, spry and stout, if she is seventy. It's up in the hills; not much of a place, but the house is clean and warm, and there's plenty of green grass, and a spring of cool water running out of the hill back of the house. The old lady wrote me that the war hadn't touched it."

"We'll find better in Mexico," said Chilton, stoutly.

Bloodgood, the Texan, who had gone for an antelope, came back in an hour, without the game but with something very much more surprising—a party of ranchmen who had been selling cattle on the Mexican border and were now returning northward with their profits. They traveled in comfortable style and had a wagon loaded with provisions, to which they invited the Ten to help themselves. They produced, too, some quinine from their medicine-chest, with which they dosed Young Hicks, and said he would be all right next day.

The two parties became so fraternal that they pitched their camp together for the night. The leader of the ranchmen, a big brown-faced man named Allen, offered to take charge of the camp until morning, and Chilton, being weary, was content, and sought sleep, which he soon found. He was awakened once in the night by the sound of men talking, so he thought, but he was so sleepy that it was merely a vague impression, and he closed his eyes again in a moment.

The ranchmen said they would start first in the morning, as they were traveling in a hurry, and when Chilton arose a half dozen of them and the wagon were disappearing over a swell of the earth.

"We'll eat our breakfast as we go along," said Allen. "Good-by!"

"We'll do the same," said Chilton, and he and his comrades mounted their horses and rode in the other direction. He was silent for half an hour, thinking, and then he said suddenly:

"How's the boy?"

There was silence for at least a minute, and then everybody looked at Old Hicks. The man was fifty years old and brown, but a flush came in his face.

"Allen said it wasn't right for the boy to go on with us," he answered, apologetically. "Besides, he was talking a lot about the old lady and the place back there on the hill. Well, he's in the ranchmen's wagon, lying very comfortable on some bags of meal, going north."

"But he swore," said Chilton.

"It don't count; he's under twenty-one," replied Old Hicks, guiltily.

The Nine rode on in silence.

Chilton presently pulled out the piece of paper which contained the agreement and scratched out Young Hicks's name.

"What are you doing?" asked Carter, the Tennessean.

"I'm keeping our names out of bad company," replied Chilton.

Old Hicks heard him, but said nothing, though the flush came again to his face.

Chilton, Bloodgood and others began to discuss the country, which had improved somewhat, but seemed very unfamiliar to Bloodgood. He believed they had wandered from the right direction, and when he examined a rude map which he carried, he was convinced of it.

"There's nothing to do," he said, "but to ride southward, and if we keep going we're sure to come to the Rio Grande at last."

Water was necessary for the night's camp, but they saw none; and taking the most conspicuous mound he could find as a center of operations, Chilton sent every man off from it in a direct line, like the spokes radiating from the hub of a wheel, each to return at the end of an hour to the hub. He did not find any, but as he rode back toward the mount at the end of an hour, Carter, coming from the west, hailed him with a shout of triumph, and Chilton's mind was at rest.

"It runs out of a hillside not more than two miles from here," said Carter.

All the others had failed, but Carter's discovery was enough.

"Hello!" Chilton suddenly exclaimed in surprise; "there are only eight of us!"

Each man looked over the little party, and then all said as if by one impulse:

"Old Hicks!"

"What's that bit of white on the hill there?" asked Carter.

Paul Dupuy dismounted and picked up a scrap of paper, held in place by a thorn.

"There's writing on it," he announced.

"What does it say?" asked Chilton.

"'Luck be with you,'" read Dupuy.

Chilton rode back a little distance in their path on the plain, and saw mixed with the hoof-prints those of one horse going in the other direction.

"He's gone, boys; we won't see him any more," said Chilton, when he came back.

"I suppose that a man has to look after his son," said Taylor, the Georgian, to McCormick.

It was a snug little place that Carter had found, a tiny rivulet spouting out of a hillside and trickling away across the prairie. After all, men and horses, had drunk from the stream, the men tethered the horses in the green grass by the waterside.

As usual, they set a watch, which Paul Dupuy was to keep the first half of the night, and Taylor the second half. It was past one in the morning when Paul Dupuy awakened Taylor and called upon him to take the relief.

"Not a bad spot, eh, Paul?" said Taylor, the Georgian, to Dupuy. "If this hill were a little higher and there were a few more trees, it might pass for a patch of North Georgia, where I used to live."

"We're going to build an empire in Mexico, and you won't see Georgia anymore," replied Dupuy.

"That's true," replied Taylor. "I never had much in Georgia, anyway. It was a two-roomed log house, and about twenty acres, I guess. There were ten acres more, but I'd been lawing over it and the case wasn't settled. That ten acres was claimed by Bill Moore, my neighbor, the meanest man that was ever born, and he went to law. The case had been going on ten years, when he enlisted in the Yankee army and I joined the rebs."

"What became of him?" asked Dupuy.

"Why, he went back there, of course," replied Taylor, "for he was too mean a man to get killed. And—thunderation! He'll be winning that ten-acre suit while I'm off building empires in Mexico."

He said not another word, but taking his rifle in hand, began his duties of sentinel and strode up and down, his eyes somber.

Chilton was first to awake, the light of a brilliant morning sun shining on his eyes.

"Up, boys!" he shouted, and then added: "Hey there, Taylor, all quiet through the night? Here, what the devil has become of Taylor? Why, the man's gone!"

"His horse is gone, too," said Bloodgood.

Chilton swore.

"What's this?" called Kidd, pointing to a tree.

Cut rudely in the soft bark of a tree with the keen point of a knife were some words. Chilton read them aloud:

"Gone to win that ten-acre case."

He looked around for a meaning, and seeing the light of understanding on Paul Dupuy's face, said, loudly and sharply:

"Well?"

Dupuy told the story of the ten-acre suit as he had heard it, for the first time, from Taylor the night before.

The brief breakfast was eaten in silence, and then they left the place, the horses turning reluctant eyes toward the green grass and fresh water. After the noon halt, Kidd, the Arkansan, rode up by the side of Chilton, who was in the lead. Chilton liked the man, who was the wildest and roughest of all the party, but who had a certain air of gaiety and humor about him. He came from a frontier portion of Arkansas near the Choctaw line, and throughout the war had been a valiant, even rash soldier.

"Will these Mexicans fight?" he asked Chilton. "I don't want to be any emperor over people who haven't got sand."

"Pretty well," replied Chilton. "My father was in the Mexican war and I've heard him talk about 'em. I guess if they're well led, they'll stand up."

"There's a crowd of fellows up in Arkansaw I'd like to have down there with us," said Kidd, reflectively.

"They'd fight, I suppose," said Chilton, with a smile.

"Fight!" replied the Arkansan, responding readily to the intended provocation. "I reckon they would! That's what they've been raised on. Why, Chilton, I fought in the feud with the Jewells before I was fourteen years old, and kept on fighting in it until the war came up and both sides went to that; and I reckon if I was back in Arkansaw I'd be fighting it again, for the Jewells will begin just where they left off, sure!"

He stopped short, kicked his horse in the side, and swore one of his choicest oaths.

"What's the matter, Kidd?" asked Chilton.

"To think of it!"burst out the Arkansan. "The feud will be raging more than ever because of its four years' rest, and me, the best fighting-man the Kidds have got, down in Mexico two thousand miles from the scenes of slaughter, building up a throne or some such fool thing for myself! Why, it's cowardice, rank treason in me!"

"Kidd, what do you mean? What are you talking about?" exclaimed Chilton, stopping his horse and reining him across the path.

"I mean that I'm going to ride straight to Arkansaw!" said Kidd, also stopping his horse. "To Jericho with Mexico and all Mexicans! Do you think they can fight that feud there in Arkansas without me? If you do, I don't. Good-by. Don't any of you boys try to stop me, because it isn't well for friends to quarrel and hurt one another!"

He waved his hand to his comrades and rode on the back track, the figure of the horse and man growing smaller and smaller until it became a mere black mark against the horizon, and then nothing.

"We are only six now," said Carter, presently; "but at any rate, we are six men loyal and true."

They began to talk again of the Rio Grande, which they hoped to reach in a day or so, and they built new castles in Mexico until they stopped for the night. After supper, McCormick produced from his saddle-bags an old and battered little accordion with which he could produce the semblance of a tune or two. With the darkness and the lone prairie as a background adding to the music a certain weirdness and a touch of soft-ness which it had not, the effect was not so bad. Felix Dupuy was lying on his blanket, the light from the camp-fire flickering faintly over his face. He and his brother were of a Huguenot family of Charleston, many generations on American soil, but still French in looks from head to heel, slim, dark and neat. Felix was the youngest of the Ten, next to Young Hicks, and the cracked music of the old accordion seemed to make him forgetful of the prairie. His brother, two years older, was watching him closely, but said nothing until the end of the fifth tune.

"We've danced by that many a time in old Charleston, eh, Felix?" said Paul.

"That's true," said Felix, "but those good old times can't come again. The Yankees have Charleston now."

"But the same people that built up Charleston before will have to build it up again," said Paul. "The dancing and the music will go on just as they did before the war. Maybe they are going on this very minute. It would be fine, Felix, to walk there again on the old Battery in the cool of the evening with the sea-breeze on your face, and see the pretty girls in white dresses with the red roses in their hair."

Chilton and Carter kept the watch that night, and when the first bar of sunlight shot up in the east, the six arose and ate their breakfast, all talking freely except Felix Dupuy, who seemed abstracted and gloomy. Then five of them rode briskly away to the south, but Felix Dupuy, the sixth, rode in the other direction.

"Look at Felix Dupuy!" said Bloodgood.

"He's left us!"

"Is your brother crazy?" Chilton asked of Paul Dupuy.

"Felix was thinking too much about Charleston last night," replied Paul, his voice full of excuse for his brother, "and he is really out of his head, like a man with a fever. If one were to talk with him sensibly, his mind would clear up and he'd come back."

"Then try it," said Chilton.

Paul put his horse to the gallop and the others remained where they were, watching the experiment. Paul rapidly overtook Felix, who seemed not to hear the galloping hoofs behind him. Chilton liked the spirited way in which the elder brother pursued the younger.

Paul rode up beside Felix and the two began to talk earnestly, as the others could tell by the motions of their heads, but the brothers, still talking, rode on, side by side, never looking back until their figures grew misty on the horizon.

"Thunderation!" exclaimed Carter. "They've both gone!"

That was the last word spoken for many hours. At the noon halt, they saw a herd of antelope on the horizon, and it occurred to all four that fresh meat would be a good thing to have. McCormick wished the honor of shooting the antelope, and they agreed that he should get the game.

He rode away in a direction somewhat to the right of the herd. McCormick was a saturnine man. He was a solitary nature. He had lived before the war far down on the Florida peninsula, on a spot of sand among the swamps, where he could bask in the warm sunshine through winter and summer alike.

That was the life that suited McCormick, who was created for a Robinson Crusoe, and when he rode off after the antelope the sun that blazed down on him seemed to him to be the same sun that he had known in Florida. He had a little hut there on the sand-spit in which he kept his guns and ammunition and skins and other small property. He had nailed up the door when he went off to the war, and as the hut stood in the wilderness, he had no doubt it was there waiting for him just as he had left it.

The wind was singing a strange tune in the blood of McCormick. He knew all the intricate country around that home of his in the Florida marshes. In a neck of woods between two swamps an old panther roamed at nights. McCormick believed him to be the biggest of his kind in Florida, and four times he had shot at him and missed. Then the war came.

"After I've become a great man in Mexico, I'll go back and see that little hut of mine and shoot that panther," he said, unconsciously speaking aloud.

He passed over a swell of earth, and it was time to dismount and stalk the antelope. He did not dismount.

"I think I'll go and see that hut now, and get that panther," he said. "As well as I can make out, that house of mine in Florida is some thousands of miles east of here, slightly by north."

He rode east slightly by north.

Chilton, Carter and Bloodgood waited a long time for the return of McCormick, or some evidence that he was still stalking the game. But the sound of no rifle-shot came to their ears; the antelope, though only dim figures against the horizon, seemed undisturbed and grazed peacefully. The three looked at one another with suspicion.

"Let's see what has become of McCormick," said Carter.

They rode toward the swell of earth beyond which he had disappeared, and there Bloodgood, who was an old plainsman, dismounted and examined the soft soil.

"He never left his horse's back," he announced, "and here goes his trail, to the east and straight away from the antelope."

It was sufficient. Bloodgood remounted his horse and the Three continued their journey southward, silent and sad.

About the middle of the afternoon, Bloodgood checked his horse and, pointing over the prairie, announced briefly that men were coming. The others were less used than he to the plains, and for a minute or two could see nothing; then they descried dimly moving figures.

"They are Indians coming our way," said Bloodgood.

The Indians rose fast from the plain as they were approaching at a half gallop. They were all warriors, at least twenty in number, gay with paint, gaudy feathers and bright blankets. Bloodgood uttered a joyful shout, and spurred his horse forward to meet the leader of the band, a large Indian with a fine presence and the features of an old Roman, to whom he gave welcome by the name of Red Dog. Red Dog knew Bloodgood, too, at once, and shook hands with him in the American fashion. Then they talked, and white and red camped together.

"Old Red Dog tells me," said Bloodgood to Chilton, "that he's started with this band on the biggest hunting-trip of his life. These men are picked warriors and hunters of the Comanche nation, and they are going to make a complete circuit after the buffalo through northern and western Texas and then into New Mexico to Santa Fe, where they'll sell the hides."

Chilton happened to be looking the other way then, and he did not see that Bloodgood's eyes were glistening. He said it was time for white men and red to part and go their ways, and shaking hands again, they mounted their horses. The Indians turned their faces toward the northwest, formed a kind of hollow square, and Bloodgood was in the center of it.

"Bid your white brothers farewell," said Red dog, with gravity and dignity, to Chilton and Carter. "He goes with us and his heart goes with us, too."

"It is true," called out the Texan, "but wherever you go, boys, I wish you luck."

The chief said something to his warriors. They burst into a long and thrilling whoop, shook their rifles, waved their lances and dashed off in a wild gallop toward the northwest, the Texan as joyous as any in the wild band.

"Well," said Chilton, looking at his comrade, "it is only you and I, Carter, Kentucky and Tennessee."

They rode into the south, sitting erect in their saddles, their faces defiant. About dusk, they selected a camp in a little grove. The night came on, thick and dark, but the fire was a red beam in its center, and the two men sitting beside it basked in its gladness and glow.

"I'll take a last look at the horses to see that they're all right," said Chilton, "and then I think we'd better roll up in our blankets and go to sleep."

He walked toward the horses, and three yards from the fire the darkness swallowed him up. He was invisible to Carter, but looking back, Chilton could see the red gleam of the coals and the dim figure of Carter sitting beside them. He saw the Tennesseean take something out of his coat and look at it a long time. When he put it back, Chilton returned to the fire.

"Carter," he said, and his voice was stern, "I'm ashamed of you, to be looking at a picture that way! You, with four years of desperate war just behind you, to be giving way to sloppy sentiment!"

"I'm not ashamed of myself," said Carter.

"Where does she live?" asked Chilton.

"In Nashville; I knew her there before the battle with Thomas."

"I guess she has married some other fellow by this time."

"I guess not; I know she hasn't."

There was a strong suggestion of defiance in the Tennesseean's manner, and Chilton did not deem it wise to say more.

When they saddled their horses the next morning, Carter held out his hand.

"Good-by, Chilton," he said. "Let's part friends."

"Going to see her, I suppose?" said Chilton.

"Yes," replied Carter; and there was in his voice a note of defiance.

"I don't think it's more than one day's ride to Mexico," said Chilton, not taking the offered hand.

"But it's very many day's ride to Nashville," said Carter, "and I must start early. See here, Chilton, we've been comrades in war a long time and we don't want to part enemies, now that we have peace."

Chilton yielded, and shook the offered hand, though reproach was in his eye.

They mounted and rode away in opposite directions, Carter to the north and Chilton to the south. Chilton never looked back. After a while, he took out a sheet of paper and tore it up; he did not want his name to be beside the others.

When Chilton said that Mexico was not more than a day's ride away, he made his time allowance too large, for by four o' clock in the afternoon he saw a yellow streak on the horizon. The streak broadened into a bar, and then became a wide, shallow river of muddy water which he knew was the Rio Grande. Beyond that yellow river lay the Mexico which was to be the scene of his triumphs. He felt emotion and urged his horse into a trot.

In half an hour he was beside the bank of the yellow stream, and two miles down he saw a tiny steamer about the size of a launch bearing the American flag. Some customs duty, thought Chilton, for smugglers were thick along the frontier.

The river was too deep to ford, but he saw a few adobe huts near by and a large skiff tied to the bank. Two Mexicans came to his hail at one of the huts and began to prepare the boat, when he showed them a small gold coin. One of them pointed to the little steamer still plainly visible on the river.

"The Yankees!" he said, in fair English.

"Yes; what business have they around here?" asked Chilton.

"None," replied the Mexican. "But they come without it. We do not like them; they are cowards, robbers."

"What's that?" asked Chilton sharply.

The second Mexican repeated the words of the first, and Chilton, flushing with anger, shouted, "Take it back, you liar!"

The Mexican drew a knife. Chilton, with a swift blow, struck him on the wrist, and the knife flew into the air. The second man came to the assistance of his comrade, but a fist driven into his face by the powerful arm of Chilton sent him head over heels. He sprang lightly to his feet and the two ran away. Chilton looked at their flying forms and rubbed his head thoughtfully.

"Thunderation!" he said. "After fighting four years against the Yankees, here I am, fighting for them!"

He mounted his horse and, riding to the highest point of the bank, gazed long at the Mexican shore.

"Well, it doesn't look like a very good country, anyway," he said at length.

Turning his horse, he rode due north.

Section II

Adventure Stories

Chapter 6

The Escape

He paused a moment at the foot of the hill, panting and weak. None of his pursuers had come in sight, and the interval was precious for rest. Yet he did not feel his exhaustion fully, until he leaned his spent and trembling figure against a rock, when every bone and muscle began to ache, and the hot breath, coming in irregular puffs, rasped and burnt like steam drawn through his throat. He strove against the growing weakness, and was sorry that he had paused, merely to give the creeping languor a chance to overwhelm him: yet he lingered, the strained heart and dizzy brain alike crying out against more exertion; then his sight grew dim, the sunlit day suddenly darkened, and he shook in a nervous palpitation as if a chill had seized him. But he was not afraid; he did not feel fear as the ordinary human type would have felt it; his emotions were physical, not mental, and with dull anger he cursed under his breath the weakness that was conquering him.

There had been many hazards in the life of Morgan, but never before had he been pressed so hard. It was a surprise and pursuit by numbers, and now he knew that only kind chance or his fleetness of foot could save him the life that he enjoyed like a strong animal or primitive man.

He leaned more heavily against the rock and his breath grew a little longer, though the pained opening and shutting of the blood valves was like the thrust of a knife. His clothing was torn into many rags by the briers and bushes through which he had rushed and red scratches were left by the thorns across his face. One scarlet line led into his mustache, from the black point of which the blood fell slowly, drop by drop, upon his chest.

A little strength returned, and with a certain coolness Morgan began to calculate his chances. He decided that they were much against him, but he had no thought save to carry the case to the final issue. He looked up at the tremulous air, the coppery sun, the bleak mountain side with its alternate rocks and bushes, and then rising, stretched his sore muscles again. As he did so he saw the tops of the bushes on the far side of the brook quivering, and he knew that if he lingered now it would be at the risk of immediate death. He paused no longer, but bending slightly over in a customary attitude of one who runs for life, and drawing his breath in deep gasps, dashed along the mountain-side. A single shout, a long yell, half a cry, half a hunting call, came from the men behind him, and all the blood flew to Morgan's head. He knew that the Jaspers, with whom the Morgans had been so long at feud, would never cease their pursuit, when chance seemingly delivered to them the best rifleman of their enemies. The opportunity his, he would not have spared one of them, and he did not expect mercy for himself.

He heard another shout behind him, half a cry of triumph, half a hunting call, and his heart swelled again with a sense of shame, felt before, when he was reminded so forcibly that he now was the hunted, and not, as usual, the hunter. He looked back and saw their heads appearing above the bushes, a dozen men strong, brown, and wild like himself, nothing modern about them save the repeating rifle of latest pattern which each carried. He perceived clearly that they were gaining upon him. In a few more minutes they would be within range. How he cursed his ill fortune in being surprised without his own rifle, and he felt that perhaps he deserved this mischance for such carelessness!

The men spread out like a fan in order to prevent his turning from a direct course, and, recognizing now the futility of such an attempt by him, Morgan kept straight on, drawing his breath with pain, and staggering often as his feet struck against a stone. The shouting of his pursuers ceased, and presently he heard a sharp report like the cracking of a heavy whip, which, taken up by the mountain, echoed through every gully and ravine until it died away under the horizon. There was a faint whistling sound, like the buzz of a bee, past his ear, and Morgan knew that the first bullet had missed him by only a few inches.

He resorted to a plan of which he had heard many speak, but which he had never thought himself to use. He began to wheel from right to left and from left to right, following a zigzag line in order to confuse the aim of his pursuers and avoid the many bullets which he knew would follow the first. The rifles cracked rapidly and he heard the whizzing of lead around him, but he was untouched, and, thankful for his agility and presence of mind, he raced on.

His attention was suddenly drawn by the familiar aspect of the ground, and he remembered now that just beyond the little slope stood the cabin of Aaron Jasper himself, the leader of the Jaspers, his flight was taking him directly towards the home of his chief enemy, but he could not turn aside now, and he plunged on up the slope, three or four rifle bullets singing around and near him, telling him for the twentieth time that it was not well to linger.

He reached the rest of the slope and there before him in the clearing on the other side stood the log cabin of Aaron Jasper-a little brown, ugly building, with its clapboard roof and shuttered windows, a light coil of smoke rising from the mud chimney.

At the sight of the cabin a fierce joy drove the despair out of Morgan's heart. The door stood wide open, and in the field a woman, who must be Jasper's wife, was working. What a triumph to use Jasper's own house, at the last moment, as a defense against him! He turned his head and sent to his pursuers a cry of defiance, a shout in which he gave them back their own taunts. Then he dashed straight for the open door with their bullets pattering around him.

Morgan slammed the door and drew into place the heavy bar that fastened it; then he fell upon the floor and drew his breath in gasps as terrible as a sob. The momentary strength poured into his brain by the reaction from death to life was gone, and the exhausted heart contracted more painfully than ever. For a moment he was blind with weakness and lay prone, his limp fingers fluttering like the fins of a dying fish. Then as his breath came back, and his will with it, he struggled to his feet and looked about him. Over the fireplace, on its accustomed hooks lay the rifle he expected. He took it down, his malignant joy swelling when he remembered that he was using not only Jasper's own house against him, but a rifle of his, too, with plenty of cartridges to supply it, ready on the mantle. Everything - the house, the rifle, the ammunition - seemed to have been arranged for his benefit, and he was duly and wickedly grateful.

Then he hastened to the single window that the room contained and, opening the heavy shutter slightly, looked out at his enemies. They had stopped in the edge of a little wood beyond rifle-shot and they seemed to be talking. Then he closed the shutter, and fastening it, looked about him again at the little fortress which had come so opportunely in his way, rejoicing in its strength and its completeness for defense. It was in its construction only an ordinary mountain cabin of stout logs, too thick to be penetrated by any rifle bullet, but the room showed some signs of neatness, though all of the articles of furniture were rude and common. He knew that this household order and cleanliness were due to Aaron Jasper's wife. A sun bonnet of hers hung in a corner, and some prints from illustrated papers were tacked on the walls.

The house, like most of the mountain cabins, had but the single room, but in one corner a small door lead to a place that seemed to Morgan to be an alcove or a large closet. He would examine it soon, but for the present he confined himself to the room. He went to the cupboard and found cold meat and bread, which he ate with an appetite increased by knowledge that he ate food furnished him by his enemy. Then he drank from the water pail, and shook himself like a great animal as the strength poured back into all his veins and muscles.

The bar that held the door was strong, but for further precaution he dragged the cupboard against it, and tearing some strips from a quilt, put a double fastening on the window. Then he opened the door of the alcove, peering until his eyes could penetrate the dusk. As the half darkness thinned and he saw, Morgan moved slightly in surprise. Varying emotions expressed themselves on his face, but presently he shut the door softly and went over to the bed. There he lay down, placing the rifle by his side and laughed long and with intense enjoyment, a kind of deep, silent laughter, internal, but expressive of the keenest delight.

He rose in a few minutes, and opening the window for the third time, he looked out at his enemies, whom he saw yet under the distant trees. His eyes caught the flutter of a woman's dress and he supposed that Martha Jasper had joined her husband and his men. If he wanted revenge on her as well as her husband, certainly he could have it. She must be half insane at that moment, and he wondered why she did not cry out and shriek to him for mercy.

He ate a little more of the cold food that he had found in the cupboard, drank some water from the pail, and his nerves felt steadier. He was about to walk to the alcove again, but when halfway stopped quite still, every nerve tingling and blood leaping in his veins. He heard distinctly a continuous shuffle and rustle like the tread of many feet and the scrap of an object against the walls. The noise increased. They seemed to be heaping something against the house. Presently he heard a faint crackle, and a belief, incredible at first, formed itself and gained strength in his mind. The crackling increased, submerging other sounds, and he knew that the warning of his fears was true. Jasper and the men had set the house on fire. He was sure of it: he could hear the blaze eating the wood and crackling in delight as it leaped from one log to another. He was as helpless as the baby that lay smiling in its sleep in the alcove. Surely it was not Martha Jasper whom he had seen in the fields, and perhaps Aaron Jasper did not know.

Yet of three things there could be no doubt—the house was on fire, he was inside it and so was the child. If he should open the door and rush out, the men waiting under the trees would fire upon him at once with an aim too good to miss. His sense of utter helplessness made him cry out, and he threw upon the bed the rifle which now seemed so useless.

The fire was increasing fast, and the rush of the flames made a roar that he heard distinctly. Shreds of smoke creeping through invisible crevices between logs, began to enter the room, and once a live spark coming in with the smoke lay for a moment upon the floor and then died.

A faint cry from the alcove drew Morgan's attention. He opened the door and looked in. The baby, a boy of two years, was sitting up and gazing at him with wide and frightened eyes. Morgan regarded the boy with a kind of malignant triumph, and found certain pleasure in seeking a resemblance to Aaron Jasper. But as he looked more closely he saw only the likeness of the child to his mother. She had been a pretty girl. He had never forgotten that. Morgan became troubled.

The flames reached the roof, he could hear the boards crackling, and smoke and sparks were coming down the chimney. The fright of the child increased, and he cried loudly. The smoke entering the room gathered in the alcove as if something drew it to that corner. A thrill of sympathy passed through the heart of Morgan. He did not like to see one so small suffer; he had been slightly mistaken in his estimate of himself. He raised the child and took him out of the alcove into an atmosphere which was a little clearer. The boy cried more loudly, the wild figure of a man adding to his fright, but ceased in a few minutes, and began to show a friendliness that embarrassed and offended Morgan. He did not want any child of Aaron Jasper's to be making a fuss over him. The boy was holding him by the collar in an attitude that was almost an embrace; he pushed off the hands, but the boy seemed not to notice the hostile nature of the act, and put them back; Morgan did not think it worth while to take so much trouble about a small matter, and let the hands remain.

The smoke crept into the child's eyes and mouth and he began to cough. Morgan found a little water in the pail and made him drink it. The heat in the room was growing intense, and Morgan wiped the moisture from his face with his coat sleeves. The little boy had become quite pale and his lips were dry; he did not cry again, but, baby though he was, gazed at Morgan with a look so full of appeal and confidence that every fibre in the wild mountaineer responded. The child must not die; his own life had become a petty thing, and he was ready to sacrifice it for the little form that clung so confidently to him.

He drew his coat over the boy's face and figure, covering him completely, while he held him in place with his left arm. The flames were running across the roof now, and burning boards fell upon the floor. He lifted the bar and threw the door wide open. A blaze of sunlight, cool, glorious, and dazzling, flashed into his face; then he saw the group of men standing under the trees with rifles in their hands. Clasping the little boy securely in his arms, he ran towards the group, a wild and frightful figure.

Some one leveled his rifle at him and some one else, who saw the burden in his arms, struck it down. Then he fell fainting at the feet of Aaron Jasper.

But the unhurt boy, pushing aside the coat, looked up and smiled.

Chapter 7

The Island Chute

"How she flies!" said Steve Boone, the pilot, to the rower in the center of the raft. "We must be beating the current by at least two miles an hour!"

Perkins, the rower, glanced down at the yellow torrent of the Cumberland, the swiftest and deepest river in the world in proportion to its length, and then up at the lofty banks that sped by, misty in the twilight. But he said nothing, merely nodding his assent. There were five men on the raft, and they never changed their positions.

The river began to curve again and to shoot around dangerous angles, and the pilot's orders now came sharp and fast. The night settled thick and black. Boone looked anxiously at the river.

"How far ahead do you cal'late it is to Corn Island?" he said to Perkins.

"Bout six miles, I reckon," replied the rower, never taking his eyes from the stream. "You take the chute to the right?"

"O' course: it's the only safe passage."

The cliffs rose higher above their heads, and the stream, narrowing, grew swifter than ever. There was a dull moaning of the wind through the forest, mingled with the angry lashing of the current on the rocks.

They whirled around a cape, dashing down the middle of the stream, and then saw ahead of them a dark object.

"Corn Island!" said Boone,

The rowers nodded.

"Pull her to the right!" called Boone, sharply, and the rowers swung the great raft toward the narrow passage around the island. Here the river was flowing swift and deep between the high bank of the mainland and the low rocky shore of the island.

The island was two miles long, and already Boone wished that he was clear of it; the channel was too narrow. Suddenly Perkins, the oarsman, a man with the ear of a hound, raised his head, and Boone saw by the light of the shanty fire that his face had turned pale.

"Did you hear that?" he asked, eagerly.

"Hear what? I don't hear anything!"

"I do! It's music, an' it's in the island chute as sure as shootin'!

The raft rushed on, sending away little waves of yellow foam, and the wind still moaned on the high bank above them. To Boone's own ears came the unmistakable sound of music, and then out of the darkness in front of them shot a great light. Behind this light loomed the shape of a river steamer, like a great white ghost. Its decks crowded with people.

"It's the *Nancy Belle*, an' we're meetin' in the island chute!"

The rowers said nothing, but their faces were white as they looked up at their leader and awaited his orders. A few minutes more and the great raft with its tons and tons of weight would crash directly into the *Nancy Belle*, which still came swiftly on. The two could not pass in that narrow channel. Boone hesitated only a moment, but in that moment all the long year's work and the glory of the great raft passed before him. The he shouted:

"Pull to the left! Pull to the left! Pull to the left!"

The river rowers, though they knew well what the command meant, pulled as if they were one machine, to the left, and the raft swung sharply at an angle toward the low shore of Corn Island. Then the powerful voice of Boone was raised again:

"Jump! Jump for your lives!"

When the raft struck with a crash upon the rocks the six men sprang for the shore. Boone fell in deep water, and when he came up again his ears were filled with a tearing, crashing sound, as the current and the rocks broke the "strapping" of the raft and sent the detached logs whirling down the river.

A log struck his left arm, and with a thrill of pain it fell useless by his side. But a hand seized him by the collar and dragged him to the shore.

"Are you hurt?" asked Perkins.

"Only a broken arm. Are we all here?"

"Yes, all here, bruised, but safe.

Up the river showed the stern light of the *Nancy Belle*, streaming safely past, and from her decks still came the soft sound of music, dying away presently in the darkness.

Chapter 8

The Lone Huntsman

"You might git over the mountain, an' agin you might n't," said Gentry, the keeper of the unclean little tavern. "There's a lot of wild and rough country atween here an' the Wood Creek Valley, an' some mighty smart men have been known to git tangled up in it. Still, there ain't no law agin tryin'."

When I left the train at Clay City, I had come by cart as far as the rough mountain roads would allow. But at last it became obvious that a wagon could go no farther, so I came on foot. The mountaineers might be in ambush for each other, but they would surely not disturb me if I did not meddle with their own pet feuds. It would be a pleasant adventure, a journey of exploration.

"Well, I'm going to make the trip," I said to Gentry. "Can you tell me how the road runs?"

"Foller the road to the creek, stranger," said the landlord. "It's there and you kin step from rock to rock. After that there ain't no road, and you kin foller your own ch'ice."

The loungers in front of the tavern gazed lazily after me as I trudged up the dusty road, and the last I saw of them they were whittling as industriously as ever. The thin, crisp mountain air expanded my lungs, and soon my muscles and nerves became firm and strong—I believed myself equal to any adventure. Though it was mid-summer and the sun was hot, the road was too stony to be dusty. The dense thickets and stubby woods that bordered the path made good shade, and I proceeded with brisk and elastic step until I reached the creek. Here I knelt and drank, and when I had crossed the stream sat down on the bank to rest before attempting the slopes that lay beyond.

As the tavern-keeper had said, there was no road beyond the creek. Apparently everybody that came this way either went up the creek or down it. I was at liberty to imagine myself an explorer if I chose—and I chose.

Selecting a stout stick as a kind of alpenstock, I pressed my way through the bushes and began to ascend the slope. The thickets did not extend far, but the ground was much broken by boulders. A mile's hard travelling brought me to the crest of the ridge, and I found that I was somewhat short of wind. If all the miles of my journey were to be like that last one, it was well that I had brought Gentry's entire supply of cheese and crackers.

The Alleghanies are not high, but no mountains impress one more with the sense of wildness, the absence of human kind. It is not the wildness of the Rockies, where trees and grass grow not, but here it is a living, breathing wilderness of vegetation, without man, the vital spark of all.

I lay down under a tree to rest a while before pressing farther into the wilderness, and while I lay I let my thoughts run back to the time when the bold adventurers from the old Eastern colonies came over these mountains into the Dark and Bloody Ground and founded the first State across the Alleghanies. To me the founding of my State has always seemed most romantic. It is past my ken how any one can fail to admire the courage of the men who shouldered their long rifles and left the fields and woods that they knew for this mighty forest-clad wilderness.

Descending the mountain was less tiring than the ascent, but it had its difficulties, and they were not a few. I found that the dwarf trees had hid from view many boulders and little steeps which opposed themselves to my passage. I could afford to neglect no precaution, lest I should fall and sprain an ankle or suffer worse. When I reached the bottom of the mountain, the sun, reaching the zenith, had begun his crawl down the other side, so I sought the densest shade I could find and lay down. Tired to the bone with hard walking, I soon fell asleep.

I was aroused by a sharp report, and sprang up in alarm, for it was my first thought that some of the wild mountaineers, engaged in the prosecution of one of their feuds, had taken a pot shot at me. But when my eyes grew a little clearer, I saw that the skies were in the blackest cloud, and a second violent crash of thunder quite as loud as that which had awakened me, followed by a bright flash of lightning, would have made it evident to the least weatherwise that a storm was coming. The lightning was so brilliant that it made me quiver. The thunder was terrifying. Soon I could see the streaks of rain across the distant sky. It behooved me to seek shelter. A large oak tree with many boughs grew near, and I found a comfortable position under it where I could sit on a stone and lean against the trunk.

A heavy wind that kept the bushes and trees bowing, preceded the arrival of the rain. Many boughs snapped before it; the edge of the wind became sharp and chill. Presently the rain came, humming in its speed and dashed about by the wind.

Cold whiffs of it were dashed under the boughs of the tree and into my face, sending the chill to my bones and making me wish that I was back at Gentry's. A feeling of loneliness and awe grew upon me.

I set my will to work to think out a plan for the night. With the earth soaking and the rain still falling, I could not sleep under a tree unless I expected to wake up shaking with a chill or burning with fever, either of which might mean death. Across one of the little valleys the mountain was precipitous and stony. I might find there a cave, or at least a hollow in the rock which would afford me shelter.

I seized my stick and ran along the mountain-side as fast as I dared. The rain had eased up a little, but the lightning seemed to know no rest. As I turned around a large rock, a tremendous blaze shot across the sky. My eyes were dazzled and then blinded. I felt a stunning sensation, as if I had been struck by a rifle ball, and fell to the ground senseless.

I do not suppose that I lay unconscious long, for when my senses returned and I struggled to my feet there was still a strong smell of sulphur in the air. But the rain and the fireworks which accompanied it alike had ceased.

My clothing was scorched. I felt strange and dizzy, and everything looked unreal. There was a roaring in my ears, but I was devoutly thankful that the bolt had done no worse.

I was in a sorry enough plight, however, for, though there were now no thunder and lightning, it began to rain again, and the need of shelter pressed upon me with increased force. I saw nothing for it but to attempt my original plan of seeking a night's lodging in some mountain cave or under some overhanging cliff, so I started again along the mountainside, though I trembled with a chill.

The clouded sun was behind the mountains and the night was coming on fast. The loneliness oppressed me so heavily that I shouted aloud, endeavoring to cheer myself. My head was still dizzy from the lightning's stroke—the mountain-tops seemed to dance the Virginia reel with each other.

At length I reached the ravine in which I thought I might find shelter. It was a deep gash in the mountain-side, and darkness lay very heavy in it. I shrank from entering the chasm, but a sharper dab of rain than usual spurred me on and I dived in. Here I found that I had improved my conditions a little. It was darker, and but little dryer than on the open slope, and in the centre of the ravine flowed a stream of water a foot deep. I stumbled into it, slipping over some stones, and fell on my knees. But the water did not increase my discomfort, for already I was as wet as I could be. I dragged myself out and for a moment thought of leaving the ravine, but concluded that I had better follow it. It led along the mountain-side like a huge plough furrow, and, keeping clear of the flowing water, and using the bank as much as I could as a shelter from the rain, I pressed along, stumbling frequently, as it was now quite dark—so dark, in fact, that I could not see objects twenty feet before me. The ravine curved upward, and in a short time I reached the summit of the low slope. I felt very weak, and my head swam around. When I managed to gather my senses together a little I made my way as best I could over the crest of the hill. Looking down the slope, I saw a point of light, and I staggered toward it, going as straight as I could; but the way was broken by huge rocks and trees, and though I tramped about from this place to that and always kept the light in view, I seemed to get no nearer to it.

For a moment I was in despair, a despair that was increased by my growing weakness and dizziness. Then I decided to shout, which perhaps would have been the better plan in the first place. I should have remembered the mountain feuds. Whoever was responsible for the light, if I proceeded noiselessly, might take me for an enemy and shoot me.

I shouted, "Help! Help!" and again, "Help! Help!" Instantly the point of light vanished. I was startled, but continued to shout. There came no answer to my cries, however, and I stopped, persuading myself that what I had seen was the phantasm of a deranged imagination.

I stood in silence for a minute or two, trying to think what next to do, and then I felt a breath over my shoulder. I shuddered convulsively and almost shrieked aloud. Some one was standing behind me, I knew, but for the life of me I could not turn to see who or what it was. All the blood seemed to gather in the top of my head and to freeze there.

"Well, stranger," said a deep voice, almost in my ear, "Who are you, and why have you been yelling here in such rash fashion?"

I turned and saw a very tall and large man standing over me. The light was too scant for me to see his face or any further detail of his appearance.

"I was shouting for help," I said. "I am lost and sick. Can you give me shelter?"

"I won't refuse to help a white man," he said. "Come along with me, stranger, and make just as little noise as you can. You never can tell when enemies are about."

These injunctions confirmed me in the conjecture that I had met one who bore a part in some mountain feud, but I could not conceive how anybody could be fierce enough for blood to hunt it on such a night.

He turned among some trees and rocks, taking a course which, as well as I could remember, led directly away from the vanished light. He walked slowly, but held his rifle before him as if he would be ready for the immediate use of it.

Again and again he changed his course. Sometimes I could make out the outlines of steep cliffs beside me, and again we were in thick woods. I had lost long since any idea of the direction in which we were going. Nor did I care. There was not room for many things then in my dazed brain. After a half-hour of such travelling my strength gave way again.

"I'm afraid I'm played out, I said to the man. "I've been knocked about so much by the storm that all my strength is gone. Then, too, a flash of lightning grazed me as it passed, and it set things inside my head to going round."

"It's not much further to my hut," said the man, "and I'll help you."

The word "hut" had a most welcome sound, for it meant shelter, and I grew stronger when I heard it. The man put his arm under one of mine, and helped me along as if I had been a little child.

"I saw a light before I began to shout. That was why I shouted," I said.

"Yes," he replied soberly, "it came from my hut, and I put it out as soon as I heard your voice. Here's the place. Come in."

We were at the door of the cabin before I saw it. The skies had brightened a little, and there was sufficient light to show a small but strong cabin, built of unhewn logs, against the perpendicular side of a hill.

"In with you," said the man.

He pushed me in and, coming in after me, quickly closed the door behind us. I heard him shoving a heavy bar in place. But I was too thankful for being out of the rain to wonder why he should be so cautious.

"Stand there a moment, stranger," he said, "and then you'll be able to see."

I heard him striking hard substances together and a feeble flame lifted up. With flint and steel he had lighted a piece of cotton wick in a pan of tallow. Next, he stirred up some ashes on a rude stone hearth and revealed a bed of glowing coals whose warmth was as grateful to me as manna to the hungry. This task finished, the man faced about and gazed at me with as much curiosity as I gazed at him.

It was a good as well as a strong face. His eyes had the look of one who is perpetually watching. His costume was antique and strange. He wore a long garment resembling a tunic made of tanned hide, probably deer-skin. It was fringed, and the fringe fell to his knees. A fur cap was on his head, and leggings and moccasins completed his attire. In the pictures of the old pioneers, I had seen men thus clothed, but I had never expected to met one in the flesh.

There were furs and skins of many kinds on the floor and walls of the cabin. On hooks on the walls were two rifles. They were like that which the man carried in his hand, very long and slender in the barrel, evidently of an ancient pattern. The cabin was dry and snug. The night was shut out. A square of board covered a small window.

"You appear to wonder at me, stranger," said the man, "but not as much, I guess, as I wonder at you."

His comprehensive glance took in every detail of my face and dress.

"You have no arms, stranger," he said.

"No," I replied; "I'm a man of peace. I never carry them."

"You're wrong there," he said. "A man should never be without them."

He looked at me a moment as if he thought I needed a keeper. But his expression quickly changed to one of sympathy.

"You do look weak and sick," he said, "and I guess the first thing for me to do is to get you something to eat. While I'm cooking it, you can dry."

He put a wooden stool in front of the coals. I sat on the stool and, taking off my coat, hung it on my knees, where it could dry more rapidly. From some recess the man brought forth several strips of meat and hung them over the fire, where they soon began to broil, the savory odor tickling my nostrils and stirring up an almost painful hunger.

"That venison came off one of the fattest bucks I ever saw," said the man. "I shot him on the mountain not a mile from here."

"I have heard that the deer are getting scarce in these mountains," I said.

"I'd like to know who told you that," he said, with an inquiring look. "I reckon that few white men besides me were ever here."

He took down a wooden platter and handed me the venison on it. I ate with a great appetite. My evident appreciation of the venison pleased him, for he smiled.

"Deer meat's not bad," he said, "when it's fat and it's cooked well. But sometimes I like a buffalo steak too."

"Buffalo steaks are scarcer than diamonds now," I said. "I guess you have to keep on wanting."

"Hardly that," he replied. "It's a long tramp, it's true, but all I've got to do is to go down out of the hills and shoot one."

I stared at him, but he looked solemn and sane.

"Deer and buffalo are not the only game you shoot?" I said.

"No," he replied; "I kill wolves, bears, panthers, and catamounts, and the Lord knows what. The woods are full of game."

I had supposed that the mountains had been swept clean of big game years and years ago. Still, the man ought to know. The fat steak that I was eating and the skins and furs piled about were proof that he did.

He went to the square of board on the wall and adjusted it a little.

"I can't afford to let the light shine through a crack there again, stranger," he said. "It was careless of me to do it before, but it may have saved your life. But them that I don't want to see might see it next time."

Evidently this was a man who bore an active part in the feuds. But he did not look bloodthirsty, nor did he resemble the shrivelled, hangdog, and back-bent race of mountaineers whom I knew. His face was fresh, and the seams in it were made by the weather, not by years.

My hunger was now satisfied and my clothes were quite dry. I felt strong, though the machinery inside my head was still behaving badly, jumping and jerking in the queerest fashion.

"Stranger," said the man, "you look better now, and I think I'll go outside and see if everything is quiet. There was a party sneaking through the country not long ago, and some of 'em may be hanging about yet. Bar the door behind me, but when you hear three knocks on it you may know it's me coming back and you can let me in. If you are attacked before I come, there are two loaded rifles on the wall."

I was about to tell him that I had no share in the mountain feuds and that surely they would not attempt to drag me into them; but before I could get the words out, he was gone. Obeying his command, I lifted the heavy bar into place and fastened the door.

Alone in the cabin, the sense of bewilderment grew upon me. I seemed to have known something of such men as this, but I could not remember where I had seen any like him.

I began to examine the cabin again. Barring the great profusion of skins and furs, it was much like an ordinary mountain cabin in the wildest parts of Kentucky. I took down one of the rifles from the wall and found that it was a flint-lock, of a style a hundred years old. By each weapon hung a great horn of powder.

Near the door and facing the path up which we had come I saw several stout pegs projecting at equal distances. I put my hand upon one of them and pulled. It came away and revealed a round hold through the wall, large enough to admit a rifle barrel.

I returned again to the stool and sat down by the fire. There was no blaze, merely the glowing coals. The wisp of smoke that arose passed up a little mud chimney and was probably lost before it reached the open air. I did not feel sleepy. Ordinarily I would have been unable to keep my eyes open under such circumstances. But now I was wide awake.

I heard three knocks on the door and promptly admitted my host.

"All's quiet, stranger," he said.

He seemed to be pleased with his reconnoissance, and, leaned his rifle against the wall, letting it go out of his hands for the first time. I noticed that the rifle was like the others, a flint-lock.

"Do you like that kind of rifle?" I asked. "Isn't it a little bit old-fashioned?"

"It's as good as they make," he replied quickly. "I never heard of any better. If anybody's got one that he thinks he can shoot further and straighter with than I can with this, let him try me."

This, then, was a genuine mountaineer who had let the world slide by him!

"I suppose you are still voting for Andrew Jackson up here?" I said, meaning to be jocular.

"Andrew Jackson? Andrew Jackson?" he said wonderingly. "I never heard of him. I once knew a man named Tom Jackson, in the Virginia settlements."

I thought at first that he in his turn was trying to have a little sport with me. But his face was grave. There was no indication of guile there. He found another stool in the corner and sat down beside me in front of the coals.

"From the North?" he asked presently.

"No," I replied.

"Thought maybe you came down from Canada," he said.

"It's a long journey from Canada," I replied.

"So it is," he said, "but it's been taken often enough. So you're not British, stranger?"

"No," I replied, wondering why he should take me for a Briton.

"I'm glad of it," he said. "They're a bad lot. They use the Indians to fight against us, and we'll never have any peace until we drive 'em all back across the ocean."

I knew that the ancient prejudice against the English still lingered in many places, but I had got pretty well rid of it myself, though it would flare up now and then when I read the histories. But I had no mind to encourage such feelings in others, seeing how idle they were at this late day.

"I have no fault to find with the British, or Canadians either," I replied. "They're like other people, some good and some bad."

"You're not a Tory, are you?" he asked. His face expressed aversion.

"Oh no," I said, smiling at his ignorance. "We don't have Tories in this country any more. I'm a Democrat."

"Umph!" he said in a tone that expressed doubt. He continued to look at me as if he failed to understand. He was silent for a while, and so was I. The burning wick in the tallow gave but little light, and the form of the big man sitting on the other side of the hearth grew shadowy.

After a while he rose, removed the board, and looked through the little window. Then he came back and resumed his seat on the stool.

"The rain's stopped," he said, "but there's no moon. I'm glad it's a black night. It makes it harder for anybody to find my house."

"You're not fond of visitors, then?" I said.

"Yours is the first white face I've seen in two years," he replied.

I wondered why he should say "white face." I knew there were no negroes in these mountains. I wondered also why he should be so careful

in watching for enemies if he had not seen any in two years. For one who
loves a feud two years is a long time between shots.

He began to look me up and down again, as if he would see from my
face whether or not he could trust me. When he had finished, he leaned
over and asked me in a low tone, as if he were afraid some one would
overhear him:

"Stranger, have you heard any news from General Washington?"

Astonished, I stared at the man. But there was not the slightest evidence of insanity about him. His clear eyes expressed the deepest interest.

"Well," I said, speaking truthfully, "I cannot say that I have had any
very late news from General Washington, but I am confident he is doing
well."

"I'm mighty glad to hear it," he said in a tone of relief. "For a while
I didn't like to ask you that question, for I wasn't sure that you weren't
one of the other side. The last white man that I saw two years ago told me
the General and his men were hard pressed. Sometimes I think I ought to
go back and help, but I like the wilderness best. I was made for it."

He was silent again for a little while, and I never thought to question
him about the strange things that he said.

"That was a great fight at Bunker Hill," he said presently, his face
lighting up. "A fur trader from the Virginia settlements told me about it.
I wonder what King George thought when he heard how his regulars
were cut up."

I said I had no doubt that King George took it very hard.

"But it will be a long fight," he said musingly. "Our people are not
organized and they haven't the arms. Nobody can tell how it will go."

I could have told the result very well, but I did not.

"Maybe you have seen something of the war?" he said to me inter-
rogatively.

I shook my head.

"Well, you don't look like a soldier, that's true," he said, "and it's a
long distance from here to where they're fighting. You're a trader,
maybe?"

I said that I had something to do with mercantile ventures. He nodded and looked satisfied.

"There's money in the fur trade for them that care for it," he said,
"but it has its risks too. I take some skins and furs myself, but just
enough to buy me powder and lead for three or four years, till the next
time I go to the settlements."

What curiosity the man may have had at first concerning me seemed to have passed away. Nor did I ask him any questions about himself. I have often wondered since why I did not, but I suppose it was because my head was so queer and jerky that night.

"If you want to sleep," he said, "you'll find a pile of skins in the corner, and they'll make a soft bed. As for myself, I'm going to do some work."

I was not sleepy then, but I thanked him for his courtesy. I moved my stool near the wall and, leaning against the logs, felt quite comfortable.

The man set about his task. From a recess he brought an armful of small bars of lead, and placed them on the hearth. He stirred up the coals again until they glowed and threw out a strong heat. In an iron ladle which he placed on the fire he melted bars of lead one after another and then began to cast bullets in a pair of small moulds.

He was as intent upon his work as an artist upon a picture. Sometimes the shining leaden pellets would drop from the moulds and roll to my feet. I would shove them back to him with my toe and he would gather up each carefully and put it in his pouch.

"I can't afford to waste my lead," he said, "for I don't know where I'd get any other nearer than the Virginia settlements. They say the British are sending guns and powder and lead to the Indians beyond the Ohio. It's a crime that they'll never get forgiveness for. White men are the only people that ought to have guns."

In order to help him, I took the pouch from him and held it. Then he would tip the molten lead into the mould, and the next moment throw the bullet out into the pouch. He worked rapidly, and the pouch grew heavy with its leaden load.

"It's a pity," he said after a while, "that some of our boys back in the colonies didn't have these to use against King George's men. I guess they need 'em bad enough. Stranger, if I had been at Bunker Hill with these and that rifle there I'd have made my mark."

He put two more bars of lead in the ladle and watched them as they slowly melted.

"Do you ever go far from here?" I asked.

"All the way to the Ohio and across it,"he said; "and I've seen some of the finest country that God's sun ever shone on. If the war was to stop and the people across the Alleghanies was to find how good the land is over here, how they'd pour across the mountains! But maybe I oughtn't to tell you, stranger, I don't want to see the hunting grounds turned into farms—not when I've come across the mountains to get away from the sound of the axe."

He looked at me with suspicion. I told him that he need fear nothing from me. This seemed to reassure him, and he turned his attention again to the bullets.

"That's ten more, he said, "twelve now, fifteen, eighteen, twenty-five. That's all, and the pouch is full. I'll take it now, stranger."

He took the pouch and put it away in the recess.

"Stranger," he said when he came back and sat on the other stool, "when you make bullets, what do you make 'em of?"

"The same as you do," I replied. "Lead."

"I mostly make 'em of lead," he said, "but I've got one here that's not of lead."

He reached his hand into the bosom of his deerskin tunic, and, producing something, placed it in my hand.

"That," said he, "is a bullet, but it's not of lead. What is it?"

The bullet shone like those that were fresh from the mould, but it had a different tint.

"It's silver, I guess," I said.

He nodded.

"It's for luck," he said. "I've carried that silver bullet three years. Everybody ought to carry one. There are some things, stranger, that a lead bullet won't touch. They are such things as are helped by the devil, but they've got no power against a silver bullet. I'm going to use this tonight."

He spoke in a significant tone, as if he were impressed with the weight and importance of what he was going to do.

"How?" I asked in surprise.

"Well," he replied, "I'm going to shoot it at something that goes on four legs; what it is I don't know, but it's more like a bear than anything else, I guess. I've shot four bullets of lead at it and never touched a hair. It never happened to me before to miss the same thing four times, and once at not more than twenty yards. Stranger, that thing was helped by the devil, and I'm going to use against it this silver bullet that the devil's got no power over."

He looked at me earnestly. Curiosity laid hold of me.

"Will you tell me about it," I asked, "and let me help you?"

"I'll tell you," he said, "but you can't help me, 'less you've got another silver bullet. 'Twould be a waste of good lead. But you can go along. I've got traps set by the beaver dam in the creek a couple miles from here, but something comes every night and takes the beavers out. I've watched four nights and shot at it, but always missed. It's past midnight now, stranger, and it will be coming. We must get ready."

He took his favorite rifle and drew the charge. Then he reloaded carefully with the silver bullet and an extra allowance of powder.

"It's not worth while for you to take anything," he said. "Only this will reach the mark."

He slapped his rifle barrel with an air of great confidence, for which I knew the silver bullet was responsible.

It was very dark outside, too dark for me to see which way I was going or along what sort of a path. But the lone huntsman trod with firm and rapid step, and I followed close behind.

For an hour or more we wound in and out among rocks, trees, and thickets, and then I heard the trickling and bubbling of water.

"This is the creek," said the hunter, "and down there in that hollow are the traps. We'll sit on this rock in the shadow of the trees and wait. Don't lean over too far, for you might fall, and it's ten feet to the bottom behind you."

He rested his gun across his knees, drew his great shoulders up a bit, and sank into an easy position, keeping his eyes on the little hollow where the beaver trap lay. I sat by his side. Though the rain had ceased long since, the forest was still wet, and we could hear an occasional drop of water slipping from one leaf and falling on another below. Looking up at the heavens, I noticed that the clouds were passing away, and it grew lighter, though the light was a somber gray.

We waited more than an hour, neither speaking nor making the slightest movement. For the first time that night I began to feel sleepy. My head nodded. My eyelids came down. I shook myself and resolved that I would not yield. The silence of the forest, broken only by the soft drip of the water from one leaf to another, encouraged sleep. Inclination became too strong for will, and, sitting erect, I slept.

I was aroused by a punch in the side. The hunter laid his hand upon my shoulder, and then pointed into the hollow. A huge bear, the biggest and fiercest that I had ever looked upon, had come into the circle of light. He held up his pointed noise and sniffed the air. But the wind was blowing toward us. The boughs of the trees arched over us and concealed us.

For several minutes the great beast stood in the hollow, sniffing and looking about. Then, reassured, he proceeded toward the beaver traps, with his head to the ground.

The hunter raised his rifle and took aim. He was very long about it, but the hands that held the rifle were steady. I looked at the muzzle of the gun, and then my eyes travelled from it to the great brute, as if I would watch the passage of the silver bullet and see where it struck. Then my eyes came back to the hunter. I saw the contraction of the muscles as his finger pressed the trigger.

The report of the rifle in the still night was doubly loud. Before its echo ceased the beast uttered a growl, half of rage, half of pain. A great gout of blood appeared upon his side. He reared up and tried to tear the wound. Then, dropping back, he turned and rushed snarling into the woods.

"It's found a mortal spot! I knew the silver bullet wouldn't turn aside," exclaimed the hunter in gleeful triumph. "He won't run more'n fifty yards before he falls!"

He sprang from the rock and rushed down the hollow in pursuit. Excited, I sought to follow. But I was incautious. I slipped backward over the rock and fell full ten feet to the hard earth, where I lay stunned.

When I recovered there was a faint streak of gray in the East. I was stiff, but I felt of myself and found that no bones were broken. Above me was the big rock from which I had fallen. I went down into the hollow in search of the hunter, but did not see him. Some great tracks in the soft earth led into the adjoining woods. But at the edge of the woods they stopped, nor could I find further trace of them.

I shouted aloud again and again for the hunter, but no answer came. The gray light in the East was giving way to the red flush of the rising sun. Then I undertook to find the cabin, but I became lost in a maze of gullies and cliffs and steep hills. Half the day I hunted for it, becoming involved deeper and deeper in the mountains. At last, abandoning a task that I now saw to be hopeless, I started again for the Wood Creek valley, guiding my course by the sun.

Chapter 9

In Sheep's Clothing

The warriors crept to the edge of the wood and gazed at the little party around the fire. They measured the distance with eager eyes, but it was too great. A rifle ball would not reach from the trees to the camp, and they must resort to some other method than a volley from ambush. Nor would they try a rush, for they knew that the white hunters never wholly relaxed their vigilance, even when they ate and told tales to one another; the bullets of their enemy might meet them before they could cross half the space.

In the dense thicket and canebrake, browning already under the breath of autumn winds, the warriors were safe, for the present, from the notice of the white men.

No eye at a hundred yards could penetrate that screen of leaves and twigs into the brown of which the brown of their own bodies blended. Hidden there they could hear the laughter and talk, and the crisp odors of the broiling venison and buffalo steaks came to their nostrils. The hunters were four in number, one young, three middle-aged; all strong and wiry, clad in tanned and fringed deerskin, beaded and ornamented in the intricate way which tells of forest vanities. They had taken the precaution to build their fire beyond gunshot of the forest, and every one held his rifle in the hollow of one arm, while he ate and talked. Even in the relaxation of the camp fire, after the day's hunt was over, they did not forget to be wary, and the leader of the hidden band saw that he, too, must use the utmost caution if he would triumph over them without loss.

The chief made a sign presently, and all the warriors retreated farther into the forest, their footsteps making no sound on the earth, the bushes failing to rustle as they passed. Then he announced the plan of action, and put the burden of it upon Palliser, the renegade.

"You will go to them, for you are a white man such as they," he said to Palliser, "and make a great rejoicing, because you find them. Tell them what tale you please about your capture by the Shawnees, your escape, and your long wanderings in the woods. Tell them no Shawnee war parties are now in Kaintuckee, and there is no danger near them. Take away their suspicions. Make them believe a good watch is not needed, and wait for us."

This was no new duty for a white renegade among the Indians, since they often served as decoys to lure the people of their own race into an ambush of the savages, though it was the first time that Palliser, who was a comparatively new man, had been chosen to do such work. But he began it with ardor, wishing to rise high in the esteem of the red men, his new people.

He scratched his face with briars until blood flowed from breaks in his skin, tore his clothing into rags, and cut great holes in his moccasins. Then he handed his weapons to the chief, who looked on approvingly at the sheep's clothing of the wolf of his tribe, and uttering a loud shout of joy rushed noisily through the bushes and canebrake toward the camp fire, repeating his cry as he ran and varying it with a wild and incoherent laugh.

The hunters sprang to their feet, rifles in hand, and looked curiously at the wretched being who approached them. Boyd, the youngest of the four, was sure that never before in his life had he seen so forlorn a specimen of humanity.

The man's long black hair hung in strings over his torn and bleeding face, and he limped painfully, stopping at times to rub his bruised feet. His rags but half covered his body, and he shouted incessantly to the hunters to help him, to save him. His whole aspect was that of a being crushed by pain of mind and body.

"A white man, and unarmed in these wilds! What has happened to him!" exclaimed Boyd, starting forward.

"Wait," said Hawkins, who was the oldest, and the leader of the four, putting a restraining hand upon Boyd's arm. "Let him come to us!"

Sutcliffe and Hines, like the other two, stood at attention with their rifles in their hands, and Palliser staggered toward them, sometimes begging for help and then joining his hands and thanking God that, at least, he saw white faces like his own. But as he came near his strength seemed to fail him.

"Help me, gentlemen! For the love of heaven, help me!" he cried. "You are white men, and I am too! I am starving, dying, help me!"

The agony upon his face was so real, so lifelike that Boyd could be restrained no longer. He rushed forward, took Palliser by the arm, and helped the bruised and battered lump of humanity to the camp fire. Palliser collapsed on a fallen log and groaned.

"Here, give him a little of this!" said Hawkins, who despite his age and years of hard life in the wilderness, was moved by the man's sufferings.

He drew a small flask, and, holding him erect, with one arm around the shoulders, poured part of the contents down Palliser's throat. The man straightened himself up, gasped a little, and the color began to come back to his face. His frame gathered more vigor. And dashing the strings of hair out of his eyes, he looked curiously at the hunters.

"Who are you?" asked Hawkins.

"Watson—Thomas Watson; at least, that 's what I used to be when I had any name," replied the man.

"How long ago was that?"

"A year or more; but I can't remember exactly; it may have been two years."

"We'll wait for the rest," said Hawkins with sympathy. "What you need just now is something to eat and you shall have it. Sutcliffe, broil strips off a hunch of fresh venison and spread them on the coals."

Palliser looked longingly at the broiling venison. He had not eaten since morning, and his hunger was not counterfeit.

The hunters thought they could see starvation in his eyes, and they felt pity.

Palliser was pleased with himself, though not showing it. He admired his own skill in the part. He believed that the chief, if he saw, would approve, and he trusted that he saw. His strength increased wonderfully. His back straightened, and his eyes became beady.

Boyd contemplated his work with pride.

"Good food will do a lot for a broken-down man," he said.

Palliser began to arrange his rags, as if returning strength brought with it a sense of pride and decency. Hawkins produced an extra pair of moccasins from his small hunter's pack and offered them. Palliser thanked him with tears in his eyes, and put on the new moccasins, throwing away the torn and ruined old ones.

"Now begin your story," said the old hunter kindly.

Palliser told how he had been taken by the Shawnees more than a year, or perhaps two years, before, for he could not remember well, he had suffered so much, and how they had forced him to run the gauntlet, beating him almost to death with sticks and switches. Then they had kept him as a slave, torturing him at times. At last he escaped from their village, beyond the Ohio, and, swimming the great river, had come into the wilderness of Kaintuckee. Here he had wandered about for weeks, not knowing which way to go. He was without weapons, and he had lived scantily on roots and wild fruit, sleeping under the trees.

"And, oh, gentlemen," he said in conclusion, "I was afraid I would never look upon a face of my own race again! When I came through the bushes yonder and saw you sitting by the camp fire, I thought I would fall dead with joy!"

The tears rose in Boyd's eyes, though the wilderness hunters, even the youngest of them, were not much given to such weaknesses.

"You are safe now," said Hawkins, "and a rest of two or three days will make you as good as ever. We'll keep this camp for a week, I guess, and what we have is yours."

Palliser thanked them again with many tears in his eyes. Then the cautious Hawkins asked him about the Indians; had he noticed any signs of them? Were their war parties south of the Ohio? No, he had seen no trace of Indians, Palliser said, and he felt sure that no war bands were in Kaintuckee, for it had been said in the village before he fled that the warriors were reserving their forces for an expected conflict with the tribes in the Northwest.

Hawkins said he was glad of it, and looked around at the great woods, rolling away for interminable miles. To him, and all his like who had wild blood in them, it would have been a happy hunting ground without a single thorn had it not been for the savages who infested it. The game had been found nowhere else in America in greater profusion and quality, and the geniality of the climate made outdoor life a continual joy.

The air had the tang of autumn crispness, and Palliser made himself comfortable by the fire, his back still against the upthrust bough, the ruddy blaze shining on his face, to which the strengthening food had brought back the good color. The hunters, too, lounged by the coals, though as usual the instinct of caution made each keep one hand upon his rifle. The patch of wood from which Palliser had come shone in the spangled glory of autumn, the reds and yellows and browns alternating. A light wind was blowing and brought with it the spicy smell of the forest.

"It's fine to be here," said Palliser, spreading his fingers before the blaze, and, for the moment, he felt the ease and peace of the wilderness. He too had wild blood in him.

Hawkins nodded an emphatic assent, while Hines and Sutcliffe looked around with an air of content. Palliser glanced toward the thicket in which the warriors lay hidden. He had keen eyes, but he could see no trace of them, though he knew they were watching every movement of his new comrades and himself. His lip curled a little with pride as he thought again how well he was playing his part.

The men had returned early from the hunt, and the sun was high when Palliser appeared among them. But it was sliding down toward the earth's rim now, and over the forest the shadows were coming.

"It will be cool tonight," said Hawkins, "and we'll let the fire burn. I'd have put it out, but since you say there are no Indians in these parts, I won't."

Then he spoke of their plans, after the week's stay in the present camp should be over. They would push on, hunting by the way, until they reached the Mississippi and when they had stood upon the banks of the greatest river, they would turn back, and make a vast curve to the south, going far down into the warmer regions near the gulf for the winter, hunting, roaming or resting as they chose.

"We'll be a year on this trip maybe," said Hawkins, "but it'll be a year that any man should be glad to have in his life."

"So it would," said Palliser, and, for a moment, his mind thrilled at the freedom and adventure of such a great and careless journey.

The red globe of the sun hung on the horizon's rim, the darkness crept over the forest, and, in the open, the twilight was advancing.

The thicket in which the still warriors lay grew misty, and Palliser could see there only a dim bank of dusk, though he knew his comrades were waiting with the patience such as they always showed in pursuit of prey. He glanced more than once at the white men to see if any suspicion appeared on their faces, but they seemed to be without care of a thought of danger and continually showed their sympathy for him. Boyd in particular was anxious for his welfare. Boyd was a fine, frank fellow not more than twenty and had been much moved by the sufferings of the man who had wandered into their camp for help.

The sun went, the night came, and all the forest was in darkness. Hawkins arranged the night watch which they always kept, even when no danger was expected. It was Boyd's turn, he said, to stand guard first and the youth told Palliser to take his blanket and wrap himself in it. Palliser did as he was bid, without hesitating, but he had a light feeling of repugnance. He did not like to accept his bed from the man whom he was about to deliver to a sure death at the hands of the savages. Then, Boyd was such a boy!

Boyd put his rifle across his shoulder, sat on the fallen log and tried to look into the darkness. The others wrapped themselves in their blankets, and their prolonged and steady breathing soon told that they were sound asleep.

Palliser did not close his eyes, though he lay quite still and listened intently. The night was dark, which suited his purpose, but he could hear nothing save the usual noises of the wilderness. Still, it was much too early. The savages, most likely, would wait until near midnight. So Palliser watched and listened. The leaves rustled musically before the touch of the wind. From afar came a faint cry like the shriek of a woman, but it was the voice of a panther. The fire blazed up and cast light around it, touching with red the motionless figures of the sleeping men. The reflection of the flame ran along Boyd's rifle barrel making a line of scarlet. The boy arose and walked in a wide circle around the camp fire looking into the darkness and seeing nothing. He came back to the fire and saw that Palliser's eyes were open.

"Not asleep yet? Aren't you comfortable?" he asked sympathetically.

"I couldn't be better fixed," replied Palliser. "But I can't sleep just yet. My nerves haven't calmed down enough."

"If I'd passed through as much as you have I guess I'd be feeling that way too," said Boyd.

Palliser looked at him with a certain liking. For a moment he was sorry that the boy made one of the party, but the feeling passed. Boyd must take his chances with the others.

The boy walked about a little more, and then sat down on the far end of the log, just beyond the circle of the firelight.

The night was slow and remained dark, clouds hiding the moon. Boyd rose presently and, making another circle around the camp, came back to the fire.

"What! Not asleep yet!" he said to Palliser.

"Yes, I slept for quite a while," said Palliser, "but I woke a few minutes ago. I am wondering just now what you men will do with me when you leave your camp?"

"That is a question," said Boyd, dropping the stock of his rifle upon the ground and leaning contemplatively upon the muzzle. "You can't go all the way to Virginia unarmed. What a pity you haven't a rifle of your own.

"What a pity!" echoed Palliser.

"I'll tell you what to do," said Boyd energetically, as if he had received a sudden inspiration. "Go with us!"

The boy's eager eyes shone in the firelight.

"Yes," he said, "go with us! Be one of us! Five are stronger than four. We'll find you a rifle somehow and somewhere, if we have to take it from the Indians themselves. I tell you, Mr. Watson, it will be worth your while! There is no life like this life of ours and we will make the grandest hunting trip that ever men undertook! I like you, and so do my comrades there, the best and trustiest comrades that ever a man had. You will never have such a chance again! Come with us!"

The wild blood in Palliser's veins responded, and he knew that his eyes sparkled. This boy had put the invitation temptingly and he half returned his liking. But he recalled his mind to the work in hand.

"No, I can't go; I wish I could and I thank you," he said, "but I must return to Virginia if I can find the way there."

Boyd was thoughtful. He made another trip around the fire and came back.

"Perhaps you had enough of wild life when you were a captive among the Indians?" he said.

"I had enough of life as a captive; but of wild life, no. I like it," replied Palliser and the last statement was true.

"And yet," said Boyd, "I hear that there are white men who have deliberately chosen a life among the Indians, and help to make war on their own people."

Palliser started and looked suspiciously at Boyd. But the boy's innocent face convinced him that it was a mere chance, these words about renegades.

"Yes, there are renegades among the Indians," he said. "I heard of them, and in fact I saw two or three."

"What could have made them take to such a life?"

"Sufficient causes I suppose, but oftenest, I have no doubt, it was crime committed in hot blood, perhaps the death of a man struck down in sudden anger, or maybe self-defense, and repented of many times afterward."

"You are probably right abut that," said the boy. "Some of them are to be pitied." The darkness did not let him see the cloud that come over Palliser's face, or the sudden softening of his look, when the boy said that some renegades were to be pitied. Palliser turned his face away from the fire and was silent.

Boyd spoke again of their great expedition into the Southwest, and the glorious hunting and exploring they would have.

"Change your mind and go with us; you will never be sorry fore it," He said.

Palliser shook his head, though the wild blood in him was leaping.

"What a pity you can't," said the boy, and his words were full of sincerity. "Good-night. You ought to sleep and I ought to be on guard."

Shouldering his rifle, he began his customary circles around the camp fire. When he had made the trip three or four times, he sat down on the far end of the log. He was motionless there, and his figure was indistinct to Palliser.

The night had not lightened, and Palliser judged that the time was at hand. The boy could see but a short way into the darkness and his watch moreover was perfunctory. He seemed to be nearer sleep than wakefulness.

Palliser raised his head a little, but with care in order that he might make no noise, and tried to look into the darkness beyond the boy. He knew that his red friends who had watched all his movements would never mistake him for the white man, and he felt no alarm on his own account.

He could see nothing, but he let his head drop back until his ear rested on the earth, and presently he heard a faint, sliding sound that made his blood quiver; he knew its cause, it was the slightest rustle; only a man creeping over the ground made that noise. Palliser looked at the sentinel who was still motionless. But it was impossible for one who did not have his ear to the earth to hear it, even when the sound grew louder.

Palliser was sorry that Boyd was on watch. Something in the boy's manner and his strong sympathy had appealed to him. There was no hope for him, as they would be sure to kill the sentinel first. Were Boyd one of the sleepers, he might be taken prisoner, and perhaps Palliser would have influence enough to save him at last and make him a member of the tribe, a renegade like himself. There had been such cases.

The rustling increased and became so distinct that Palliser, with his ear to the earth, could tell that it proceeded from the thicket in which the warriors had lain hidden, and was coming directly toward the dozing sentinel. The sound was that of a long body drawn softly over the earth. Palliser looked at the older men. Their faces were fixed and they slept soundly, drawing long and regular breaths. They would not waken until the shouts or blows of the warriors aroused them. Palliser turned over two or three times and came a little nearer to Boyd, where he could see better. He made no noise and the sleeping men slept on as peacefully as ever. A straggling moonbeam fell on Boyd's face and showed his drooping eyelids. He was at least half asleep and the vigilance that he might have preserved through habit seemed lost in some memory that made his lips curve into a smile. Palliser felt sorry more than ever for the boy.

He could hear the sound of the sliding body now, without placing his ear to the ground, and presently he saw a darker line upon the surface of the earth. The creeping warrior was coming near, and Palliser felt sure it was the chief, himself, for the would wish the honor of striking down the sentinel.

The warrior crept nearer and he could see that it was, in truth, the chief, ready with his knife to slay the dreaming boy. Surely Boyd would awake and make a fight for his life!

Surely he would hear the leaves and grass rustling behind him! But he did not stir, though the moonbeam played over his face, as if it would warn him. Palliser trembled under the tension of his drawn nerves. The boy ought to have a chance. He rolled over again, and purposely kicked one of the burning pieces of wood. It fell with a plunk into the ashes, but neither the sleepers by the fire nor the boy heard, only the warrior.

Palliser could see the eyes of the savage gleaming in the dusk, as he stopped and crouched down at the noise. Then, when it was not repeated, the chief crept on again, until he lay on the ground just behind Boyd and within striking distance.

Palliser gave up hope. The boy would never hear now. The chief rose to his feet with his ready knife, and Palliser could see upon his face the malignant play of his passions.

"How easily I could prevent this if I wished to do so," thought Palliser. "I would have only to reach my hand toward the rifle of one of these hunters."

As proof of the thought the hand moved toward the rifle. The chief stood erect, towering over the sitting boy, and after the manner of his race prolonged his enjoyment, looking down at the unconscious figure.

Rising impatience and anger filled the mind of Palliser. He was seized with a great repugnance for this Indian habit of gloating over a victim. He had never before seen the chief look so evil. His hand touched the rifle and the cold steel of the barrel felt good. Mechanically, his fingers crept toward the hammer and trigger. The chief raised the knife, and Palliser's fingers closed around the rifle.

Higher went the knife. The moonbeam that had played over the boy's face deserted him and shone on its blade. It was about to strike, but a rifle was fired, echoing in the night, and the chief fell, shot through the brain.

"Up, men, up!" shouted Palliser, in a wild delirium of excitement. "It's an Indian attack, but I've killed the leader, and we can beat 'em off!"

The savages rushed from the bush, but, disheartened by the fall of their chief, and surprised when they expected to inflict surprise, they were quickly beaten off and fled in the darkness.

The battle over, Palliser leaned against a tree, pale and trembling.

"Here are the rifle and ammunition that you needed," said Boyd, handing him the equipment of a fallen warrior. "You're a brave man and you've saved all our lives. We ask you again to go with us."

"Do you really want me?" asked Palliser.

"Yes," said all.

"Then let us go," said Palliser, his eyes shining as the firelight played upon them. The five took up their light packs and, walking in Indian file, one close behind another, disappeared in the great Southwestern forest.

Section III

Autobiographical Essay

Chapter 10

What the Home-comers Saw*

It has been charged often by the West and the South that the New-Yorker lives in a little world of his own, and neither knows nor cares what the rest of the country is thinking and doing. If a New-Yorker will take the trouble to visit the West or the South he will find that the charge contains a large percentage of truth.

The State of Kentucky, which is of both the West and the South, just inclining more largely to the latter, has just given a home-coming week to the half-million or more of sons and daughters who have wandered from the land of their birth, and among those who returned for a brief stay were a number who have lived long in New York.

These New-Yorkers as soon as they crossed the Alleghany Mountains, whether at a Northern or a Southern point, seemed to breathe a different atmosphere and to come into contact with a wholly fresh and buoyant spirit. In New York the talk was all of graft, of corruption in government, corporation, and individual. Insurance companies were rotten, one who ate Chicago meat ran the risk of cannibalism, the papers swarmed with accounts of crime, and every day in the metropolis three or four recently imported Italian gentlemen were killed by other recently imported Italian gentlemen. Englishmen and Scotchmen were writing to the press, telling how they ordered things better in Great Britain, and one who did not carefully preserve his sense of proportion was likely to despair of the republic. Americans in New York cowered before Euro-

* *Harper's Weekly*, 50 (July 28, 1906), 1073.

pean opinion, and the reading classes wondered what Henry James was going to say next about us.

Beyond the shadow of New York the change was quick and absolute. The home-comers were once more in indomitable, optimistic, republican America, republican to the core, prosperous as it never was before, happy in the present and expecting a greater happiness in the future. They saw in Ohio and Indiana and Kentucky a beautiful land, vastly improved in a few years, better homes, better fences, better railroads, and bigger and better towns, country and towns alike peopled by a sturdy, handsome race.

Everywhere, too, in this mighty Mississippi Valley, the largest and most fertile continuous body of land the world has to offer, manners and morals are improving. Hard drinking has practically ceased, and fighting is going the same way. In Kentucky I saw fifteen thousand people gathered to welcome the home-comers, and to eat dinner on the grass in the old-time fashion. In all that crowd there was not a single intoxicated person nor was an angry word spoken by anybody.

What pleased the home-comers most was the intense American spirit throughout the whole valley, and this American spirit was the finest thing there. It showed itself in the pride that the people have in their own country, and their confidence that it is the best. Nearly all who can afford it go some time or other to Europe, and they generally return with the opinion that the Old World is overrated both in the picturesqueness of its past and the cheapness of its living. I ate a better and better-served dinner in Louisville for fifty cents than I was ever able to find in Europe at the same price.

The people, too, were more American in looks as well as in spirit. There is a great new hotel in Louisville, and everybody passes through it. As I sat in the lobby with old friends I was proud of my countrymen. I saw a finer-looking crowd than one ever sees in New York, taller, fairer, and cleaner cut of feature, both men and women. This was the native stock; it was not pulled down by the floods of a darker and more stunted growth that Europe is pouring upon New York. In common with the other home-comers I felt with renewed force what a lucky thing it is for the average man to be born an American.

The home-comers returned to New York with increased optimism and fresh inspiration, drawn from the mighty West and South, the republican heart of America.

About the Author

R obert M. McIlvaine received his Ph.D. in American Literature from
Temple University in 1972. Since then he has been an English Pro-
fessor at Slippery Rock University, teaching American Literature, Cre-
ative Writing, and composition. He has published articles on many American authors, including Edgar Allan Poe, Stephen Crane, Theodore Dreiser,
Eugene O'Neill, Ernest Hemingway, F. Scott Fitzgerald, Edith Wharton,
E.E. Cummings, Wallace Stevens and others.

For the last five years he has been researching the life and works of
a favorite boyhood author, Joseph A. Altsheler. While neglected today,
Altsheler was probably the most popular boys' author of the first half of
the Twentieth Century, and McIlvaine was gratified to discover on re-
reading that Altsheler was as good an author as he had remembered.
McIlvaine has published several articles on Altsheler, and his ambition is
to restore Altsheler to his deserved place in American Literature.

www.ingramcontent.com/pod-product-compliance
Lightning Source LLC
Chambersburg PA
CBHW030654110726
47901CB00002B/705